She didn't make a sound...

She twisted and struggled. Morgan didn't enjoy holding Delia so firmly. He had simply wanted to talk to her, try to make her understand what he was feeling. Putting his feelings for this woman on the line frightened him, but he couldn't stand the tension. It was time they settled their relationship once and for all.

Morgan eased Delia up against the barn wall. The bright light from inside spilled across her face as she looked up at him with a strange expression. Defiant. Yet vulnerable.

He studied her face, remembering other places, other times: her eyes, wild and excited by passion; her lips, swollen from his kisses; her cheeks, flushed with the aftermath of their lovemaking.

Without really knowing why, he lowered his face to hers.

ABOUT THE AUTHOR

Elda Minger became a writer via a circuitous route. Through the years she has worked in several bookstores, cleaned houses in Beverly Hills, ushered in theaters, sung for her supper on Hollywood Boulevard, and even appeared in two movies. Born and now residing again in Hollywood, California, Elda has lived in many parts of the United States, as well as in such foreign countries as Italy.

Books by Elda Minger

HARLEQUIN AMERICAN ROMANCE
12—UNTAMED HEART
95—ANOTHER CHANCE AT HEAVEN
106—TOUCHED BY LOVE
117—SEIZE THE FIRE

These books may be available at your local bookseller.

Don't miss any of our special offers. Write to us at the following address for information on our newest releases.

Harlequin Reader Service
P.O. Box 52040, Phoenix, AZ 85072-2040
Canadian address: P.O. Box 2800, Postal Station A,
5170 Yonge St., Willowdale, Ont. M2N 6J3

Seize
the Fire
ELDA MINGER

Harlequin Books

TORONTO • NEW YORK • LONDON
AMSTERDAM • PARIS • SYDNEY • HAMBURG
STOCKHOLM • ATHENS • TOKYO • MILAN

In memory of my father, Ralph,
who always encouraged my dreams.
And for my mother, Julia,
who set me a courageous example
and showed me how to attain them.
This book is dedicated
to both of them, with love.

Published September 1985

First printing July 1985

ISBN 0-373-16117-4

Chapter One

What am I doing here?

He'd asked himself the question countless times during the last two hours.

It's too good a part to pass up.

No, he corrected himself. *You wanted to see her again. After six years you still jumped at the chance.*

Everything always came back to Delia. As he sipped his drink and eyed the crowded room, he watched her carefully, studied her, drank in the sight of her. Reality was so much better than all the nights he'd dreamed of Delia.

She'd turned into a beauty, but hadn't she always been beautiful to him?

She's so nervous. And thinner than I remember.

He'd been following her with his eyes for the better part of the evening, waiting for a chance to talk with her. Alone. What he wanted to say couldn't be said with people around.

She was skimming along the edge of the room, and when he saw where she was headed, he smiled.

The balcony. How perfect. How ironic. His Juliet.

Setting down his drink, he walked purposefully toward the glass door.

Time to play your hardest part, Buckmaster. A man who doesn't care.

THE SURROUNDING PEACE and serenity couldn't have been more at odds with the way Delia felt inside.

She stood on the balcony of her father's Malibu beach house, her eyes focused on the gentle ebb and flow of the Pacific. The night sky was illuminated by a full moon, its reflection dancing over the waves as if in silent mockery of her plans.

Whatever had possessed her to think of Morgan Buckmaster for the part?

She tightened her fingers on the redwood railing as she heard the glass door behind her slide open.

"I thought I'd find you out here," the deep masculine voice murmured. His accent was soft, perfectly mid-Atlantic, with crisp vowels and consonants. An actor's voice. And Morgan Buckmaster was one of the finest actors in the world.

Delia kept her back to him. The salt-scented breeze whipped her hair against her cheeks. She didn't want him aware of her feelings. Morgan was expert at searching people's faces to discover whatever emotions played across their features. The gift of an actor.

"Aren't you going to talk with me?" He sounded slightly annoyed.

She took a deep breath and faced him.

"What is it you want to talk about?" she asked politely, hoping her eyes would freeze him.

"You."

Delia felt her eyes widen. She nervously moistened her lips. Damn Morgan! He was moving too fast. She didn't like the feeling.

She turned slightly away and concentrated on the ocean below. But what could he do to her here on the balcony? Beyond the glass door people were talking and laughing. They weren't alone.

"What about me?" She attempted to sound casual.

She felt him move behind her; then he was standing at the rail. Too close. She didn't want to turn, didn't want to see the way his body moved. Gracefully. Instinctively. There was something uncivilized about Morgan.

"You've become a beautiful woman, Delia."

"Thank you." Barely civil, she was tempted to lash out verbally. Delia had no desire to discuss her looks with him. Yet she had to remain polite, detached, if only for her father's sake. But she had to get away from him.

She swallowed against the tightness in her throat. "I'm going to get something to drink. Would you like anything?" She was halfway across the large balcony when he spoke.

"You aren't afraid of me, are you?" There

was a strange quality in his voice. She couldn't quite define it.

Delia turned in mid-step, trying to control escalating emotions. For one instant she considered telling him the truth. But the second the thought flickered through her mind, she knew she wouldn't. James was too private a man.

"I'm not frightened of you," she stated flatly.

"Good." Morgan patted the rail beside him. "Come back and stand beside me for a minute. Then, I promise you, we'll go inside."

She had walked into his trap. Delia hesitated.

His eyes darkened, and his voice grew softer. "Come here, Delia."

She was already moving in his direction, as helpless as a mouse against a cobra. Then she was beside him, grasping the rail and looking out over the calm Pacific below. Lights from the first floor of the beach house illuminated white foam breaking against smooth sand. Delia remembered playing on that stretch of beach as a child, making sand castles, dancing in and out of the waves, shrieking with happiness.

She tensed as she felt his hand close over hers. Her stomach knotted in anticipation of promised pleasures. Morgan slowly raised her hand to his lips. They felt warm against the inside of her wrist. She made a small, ineffectual pulling motion. But he laced his fingers through hers and held fast.

She glanced up. Once his gaze caught hers, she couldn't look away. The sensuous dark eyes she'd seen so many times in her dreams were studying her face, assessing her. Delia wanted to break free, to run back to the safety and noise of the party. But she couldn't.

"You have the softest skin," he murmured, pressing another kiss into the tender center of her palm. "Rose Red, that's who you are."

"What?" She tried to reply, but the sound came out a strangled noise.

"Rose Red and Snow White," he explained, as if telling a story to a child. But he wasn't condescending. "Rose Red had hair the color of ebony and skin as white as ivory."

Delia thought wildly that any other man would have made the same speech ludicrous. She could have burst out laughing, walked easily away.

But Morgan made her believe.

"Eyes as blue as periwinkles," he breathed, moving closer. "And lips as red—" his mouth was a heartbeat away from hers "—as a rose."

His lips touched hers gently, sensually. They were warm and firm. Experienced. Delia's legs started to shake as she bloomed sensually beneath his touch. Morgan moved his hands over her bare back, fingers lightly caressing. His touch told her far more eloquently than words of his sensual power over her.

A heated weakness suffused her body, and Delia longed to give in to pure sensation, letting Morgan take her higher and higher.

His hands touched her silk-covered hips and pulled her against him tightly, making her aware of his hard masculine strength, the clean scent of his cologne, the warmth of his body, the way he reached up and gently threaded his fingers through her hair.

His lips teased hers apart, deepening the kiss, making her aware of his desire. She felt his tongue move inside her mouth with expert ease, urging her response, making her want to put her arms around his neck and let him lead her into pleasure. But she couldn't. Not this time. Not again.

Delia tried to wrench herself away from his grasp. What was she thinking of? His fingers, laced through her hair, coerced her to turn her face to his, made her bend her head back so his lips could kiss her neck and move lower still, to the slight shadow between her breasts.

Somewhere, as if in a very distant dream, she heard a glass door slide open. A deep voice boomed out, "Come on; we're ready to cut the cake!"

Morgan finally released her. He was breathing deeply, his dark eyes burning as if lit by an inner fire, watching her.

She turned away from him, furious at her earlier response. Running a shaking hand through her tumbled hair, she silently acknowledged his mastery. Morgan still affected her as no other man could.

"Cordelia." His deep voice was soft in the darkness, almost a caress. She glanced quickly over her shoulder.

Morgan surprised her. After the way he had just kissed her, she would have expected him to have a hard, victorious expression. But the dark eyes were still watchful. Did she detect sudden pain in their depths, or was it what she wanted to see? She backed away, then ran to the sliding door, shutting it sharply behind her.

She stumbled slightly as her feet made the transition from hard redwood planking to the soft carpeting of the living room. Her father's guests were by the large oak buffet table where a tiered cake glittered with sparklers.

Delia didn't feel safe until she locked the bathroom door. Her knees were still shaking. She sat down on the edge of the tub and put her head in her hands. What had happened out on the balcony couldn't have happened!

But it had.

He was stalking her, playing with her the way a cat did with a mouse. She put her hand over her heart, as if the simple gesture could silence its racing. How could Morgan still have this effect on her?

It had been years since their last fight, years since she had walked out of their flat in London, slamming the door behind her with awful finality. Yet the attraction she'd felt for him out on the balcony was as potent as if they'd been separated only that morning.

Morgan still had power over her, and she wasn't at all happy about the vulnerable position she was in. If she had only herself to consider, she would have left the beach house and run as far away from him as possible. But her life wasn't that simple now.

As soon as her legs steadied, she got up and

walked over to the large mirror above the double sink. Her lipstick, a bright slash of deep plum on her pale face, was smeared. Reaching for a tissue, she wiped it off. She searched through a drawer and extracted a brush. The bristles dug into her scalp as she ran it through her hair, restoring order where Morgan's fingers had been.

She had just returned the brush to the drawer when she heard a knock on the door.

Morgan?

"Delia, are you there?" It was Mary, her stepmother.

"Yes, just a minute." She checked the mirror quickly. Taking a few deep breaths, she opened the door.

Delia found a small measure of comfort in Mary's familiar features: her short gray hair and kind brown eyes; her tall, slender body. She wondered if her stepmother had seen any of what had happened on the balcony. Sometimes Mary could be too perceptive.

"Your father is asking for you, darling. He won't cut the cake until we're all there."

She nodded, then stepped out into the hallway and followed Mary.

Though the dinner party had been small, the living room seemed quite crowded. All the guests were gathered around James Wilde, who was standing in back of the table that held his seventieth birthday cake.

"There you are!" He was clearly glad to see his daughter. "I was looking for you."

She smiled, her expression softening as she

looked up at her father. James Wilde was a big bear of a man with a heart as soft as a child's. When Delia had been small, she had worshiped him. Now, many years later, she still loved him with all the intensity she'd felt as a little girl.

She maneuvered her way through the guests until she stood at his side. "Do you want me to help you?" she asked softly.

He shook his head, frowning. "Mary's getting out the champagne. Why don't you help her?"

As she started toward the kitchen, she was aware of someone watching her. Scanning the room, she saw Morgan leaning against the far wall. When their eyes met, he lifted his drink in a silent salute.

She escaped to the kitchen.

Though Delia had resented Mary as a young child, as a woman of twenty-eight she could understand that her stepmother suited her father much better than her mother. The love between James and Mary Wilde was rare and wonderful to watch.

"Where's the champagne?" James bellowed. The two women smiled at each other.

"He's always so impatient." Mary picked up two bottles.

"And you love it," Delia teased.

"Has James talked to Morgan about the film?" Mary whispered, making sure no one could hear.

Delia shook her head, carefully keeping her facial expression calm.

Mary smiled. "James likes him. I can tell. I think Morgan will agree to—"

"Mary, we're waiting!" There was a hint of humor in her husband's voice.

"I'm coming," she called, then turned her attention back to Delia. "You'll have to talk to Morgan soon."

"I know. I will." As soon as Mary left, Delia leaned back against the counter.

Had it only been three months ago she'd thought everything in her world was secure? Now the only thing that mattered was her father. And getting the film done.

She picked up two more bottles of champagne and forced herself to walk into the crowded living room.

James had made the room the favorite area of the entire beach house. It was expensively informal, with plush sand-colored carpeting and a west wall composed entirely of windows. The view of the ever-changing Pacific was magnificent. There were no curtains to shut out the sky—deep velvet studded with stars. Two leather sofas were placed opposite each other in front of a large stone fireplace. On the mantel rested three Oscars, silent testimony to James's acting career. Warm cream walls were almost entirely covered with photos. Delia as a child, James and Mary on the ranch, James with actors and directors from all over the world. But there were far more family pictures than professional photos.

Her glance flitted restlessly over the walls. James on Falstaff, his prize quarter-horse stallion. James and Mary on their wedding day, on horseback, of course. Delia on her first pony, smiling a toothy grin. Endless photos of dogs and cats. The mountains that surrounded their ranch in Wyoming. But most of all, the people in the pictures. Mary laughing. Delia clutching her father's leg. She must have been all of three when that picture was taken.

An entire life was captured on those walls.

The cake had been cut. James was seated on one of the large leather sofas with Mary, opening presents. His delighted roars of laughter filled the room. The sound tore at Delia's heart. She stared at her father, her vision blurring.

"Do you need any help?"

Her eyes slowly focused on Morgan's dark face. He used to know her emotions so well. How much had he seen revealed in her face?

"Here." She thrust the two bottles she was holding in front of her. Delia watched as his large hands closed over the frosted glass. She averted her gaze.

"Have you thought about the film?" she asked, trying to distract him from reading her expression too closely.

He seemed surprised. Delia tried not to look away as he studied her face. What did he see there?

"Cordelia Wilde. Always the dutiful daughter, aren't you?" His face relaxed slightly.

Delia tried to curb her impatience. It was difficult. Much as she didn't want to work with Morgan, she knew James had his heart set on Morgan playing the second male lead. She was also aware that Bob Rosenthal, the film's producer and an old family friend, had already talked with Morgan.

He was still studying her in that curious way of his. Did all actors go about their scrutiny quite so rudely? Yet there seemed to be something else in his guarded expression that disturbed her. Possessiveness? But that was ridiculous. Morgan had made it quite clear what he thought of her during their last fight in London, so long ago.

"Let's get the champagne out before it gets warm," he said.

He was as good as his word. A short while later Delia found herself on the other end of the sofa with Morgan. He always seemed to take over and direct things before anyone else had a chance. While this trait was going to make working with him very difficult, part of her found his strong presence comforting. She needed someone to lean on tonight.

"This is quite good." His voice broke into her thoughts as he gestured toward the cake with his fork.

"Thank you."

He seemed surprised at her response. "Did you make this?"

She nodded, taking a taste herself. Her chocolate cake, James's favorite. Deep and rich, with bittersweet chocolate frosting, decorated with chocolate leaves. A small china quarter horse reared on the top layer. Everything had to be perfect for her father.

"I'd forgotten what a good cook you are," he

murmured softly, his lips close to her ear. "Do you still make fettuccine Alfredo?"

The seemingly casual remark sent a wave of hot color up her neck. Delia set her fork down. Unbidden, memories of late-night suppers with Morgan flashed through her mind. She could visualize perfectly their small London flat and remember her feeling of excitement as she heard his footsteps on the stairs. Morgan knew exactly how to push the knife in and twist it deliberately until it hurt like hell. He knew as well as she how most of those suppers had ended. In bed—

"What is it you do, Delia, besides lie out on that balcony and sunbathe?" The remark could have been cruel, but his tone wasn't.

Delia yearned to share her emotions with him—her excitement and fear over her part in the film, her feelings about her father. But her cautious, reluctant side remembered emotional pain at his hands, his indifference to her career as they had both struggled to pay their dues. And the way he had felt about James. Morgan was too proud, sometimes.

She pushed her hair back from her forehead. The room seemed unbearably hot and crowded. *I live from day to day and try to believe life will get better.* She paused for a moment, praying that when she replied, her voice would be steady.

"I'm a director."

His dark eyes widened a fraction. He hadn't expected her answer. Then amusement filled his face. At that moment, Delia wanted to hit him.

Why did Morgan have to provoke such a violent response in her?

"Everyone in Hollywood wants to direct. What is it you really do?"

His complete refusal to take her seriously made her see red. Anger flowed through her, quick and hot. And it was at that exact moment that Delia realized how furious she still was with Morgan. How much unfinished business still remained between them—almost like another woman. She fought back the impulse to push her piece of cake into his handsome face. Without a word to let him know how much he had hurt her, she stood up and walked away. Morgan Buckmaster could go straight to hell—with her blessings.

She spent the rest of the evening by her father's side, surrounded by his old friends. Most of them had known her since she was a baby. Delia wanted the comfort familiar people offered. Not that dark, annoying man.

Later in the evening he approached her again.

"Did I offend you with my remark?" he asked, his eyes expressing his disbelief.

"No," she answered coldly, wishing her tone of voice wouldn't give her true feelings away.

"How many films have you directed?" He seemed interested.

"Three."

"Big budget, were they?"

"Listen, you—"

But she was interrupted as Bob Rosenthal swept her into a hug.

"How's my girl?" Bob was almost the comic

opposite of James. Tall and thin, he looked as if a good wind would blow him away. His lean, tanned face was open and trusting among friends. But Delia had seen him negotiate within the film industry. She knew he could be cold and calculating when it served his purpose.

Bob stepped back, pretending to examine her. She smiled. He had just been over to dinner the other night. "Lovely. The image of your mother."

She was uncomfortably aware of Morgan watching the entire exchange.

Bob gave her a quick kiss on the forehead, then turned his attention to Morgan. He didn't waste any words.

"Good evening, Mr. Buckmaster. Have you decided whether or not you're signing on?" His tone was friendly, yet firm.

Morgan looked him straight in the eye, his dark glance impassive. "I think so, I've always wanted to work with James Wilde, and the script was brilliant. I've never been fond of Westerns, but this one seems special."

Bob was pleased. "Then you'll be down at my office on Monday?"

Morgan nodded. His expression altered slightly. Delia could read his mind like a computer printout as he glanced quickly from Bob's arm around her shoulder to her flushed face. The connection he was drawing between her earlier declaration about her career and her relationship with Bob was obvious.

His next question was spoken in a quiet tone of voice, but his eyes remained on her face.

"Who's directing?"

Bob seemed surprised. "Didn't James tell you?" He turned toward Delia, then looked back at Morgan.

"Delia is directing."

With confirmation of his suspicions came his anger. The signs were minute, but they were there. Delia knew Morgan was furious. The skin around his mouth whitened, and a muscle tightened in his jaw.

Yet he had too much business sense to lose his temper in front of Bob. Couching his features into an expression of cold politeness, he shook Bob's outstretched hand. "I'll see you on Monday. And thank you."

He caught her eye. "Cordelia, could I talk to you for a moment?" The polite words hid his furious temper.

She was about to refuse when his fingers closed over her wrist. She nodded and allowed him to pull her gently away from Bob.

Once they were out on the balcony, Morgan got straight to the point.

"Why the hell are you directing this picture?"

Delia almost flinched at the angry expression on Morgan's face. The bright moonlight highlighted the sharp angles and chiseled planes, the strong jaw. In a part of her mind she realized he really was a beautiful man.

She thought once again about telling him the truth. As she watched the muscle in his jaw tighten, she thought better of it.

"It's a major step in my career," she replied

flippantly. At the astonished look on his face, she laughed. Delia was amazed at how calm and carefree she sounded. "Surely you can understand that?" She felt much more in control of the situation. At least she knew the business.

His hands gripped the railing, knuckles white. But she wasn't afraid of physical violence. Morgan had told her more than once he detested men who hit women. Their fights had been verbally intense, but he had never touched her in anger.

"Isn't it really just a matter of letting Daddy buy you a film?" His tone was cutting, meant to wound.

Delia couldn't see for a moment, could hardly breathe, her anger at Morgan was so intense.

She was about to reply when he cut in. "It's the director who makes the film, supervises the editing, helps the actors find their best performances. Why should I want to risk my career to a nepotistic little manipulator like you?"

Delia's hands trembled. She clenched them into fists. And yet, in the midst of her anger, she could see his point. The three films she'd directed in her career had been low budget—and not very well distributed. She doubted Morgan would have seen them in England. It was obvious to a child she wouldn't have been given this opportunity if she wasn't James Wilde's daughter.

But wasn't that exactly why she was doing this film?

She couldn't tolerate any more of this; she was losing patience with both herself and him. Feeling like a stranger toward him, she smiled sweetly. A rage she hadn't known she possessed kept her voice calm as she said, "I guess it's just a matter of take it or leave it, isn't it?" Though she hated to do this to James, she wanted Morgan's final decision before the night was over. While Morgan might just walk out at her ultimatum, the odds were on her side that he'd want to compromise. He wanted this film. He wanted to work with James, and he wanted everything that went with it. Delia held her breath as she watched him whiten even more. Morgan Buckmaster wasn't going to be an easy adversary.

He turned away from her and began to walk toward the glass door. She felt her heart hammer painfully in her chest. Delia knew she'd lost. She had goaded him too far! Morgan was a proud man. The time she'd lived with him had proved that. Now he was walking out on her again. And the picture.

She forgot her earlier reluctance toward working with him and began to follow his rigid back. Before she reached him, he turned. It was as if he impaled her with a glance.

"I'll see you tomorrow at noon," he said abruptly. "At my house, for lunch. We'll discuss this—" he searched for a suitably scathing word and found one "—fiasco when you get there." And without a backward glance he slammed the glass door shut behind him.

Delia held on to the railing tightly, her shoulders slumped. All her energy left her when Morgan exited. But he was still willing to talk to her.

Maybe she hadn't lost. Maybe she still had a chance.

Chapter Two

Delia was almost asleep on the chaise longue when Mary stepped out on the balcony.

"James is fine," she said immediately. "I've got him settled for the evening." She sat down on a white canvas chair. "Thank you, Delia."

"For what?" She sat up, tucking her feet underneath her.

"For the party. For finding the script, and all your endless talks with Bob. For making sure the entire film will come together." She paused before her last statement. "For facing Morgan again."

Delia sighed. She leaned back against the chair. "I was surprised he accepted your invitation." She avoided her stepmother's eyes. "I'm going to have nothing but trouble with him." Delia suddenly realized one of the reasons she loved Mary so much was that you could tell her anything and she would never judge you.

"I thought as much," the older woman replied, looking out over the sea. "He was watching you throughout the party—but then you were aware of that, weren't you?''

Delia nodded. "Oh, he's quite hot on getting me back in bed again. He just doesn't think I can direct worth a damn." She was surprised at the bitterness in her voice. It wasn't as if she hadn't run into opposition before.

Mary smiled. The expression made her features appear less strained. "He's still a man."

"I'm not disputing that!" Delia exclaimed. "I just wish he'd leave well enough alone and agree to do the film." With Morgan gone for the evening, she was able to put her emotions in perspective and think of her father. Acting with Morgan Buckmaster would be a fitting final performance in James Wilde's long and brilliant career.

"Oh, he will." At Mary's calm response, Delia stared at her.

"How can you be so sure?"

"He'd be a fool to refuse. The script is better than anything he's done in several years. Working with an actor like James will give him a chance to stretch himself. Opportunities like this don't come very often for an actor with his talent." She took Delia's hand and squeezed it gently. "He's made very smart career moves. I can't see the pattern suddenly changing." Her voice softened slightly. "And Delia, I appreciate what you're going through. It can't be easy, seeing him again after all that passed between the two of you."

Delia felt tears sting her eyes. Mary knew everything. She'd taken care of her when she'd flown back to the ranch, heartsick after the breakup with Morgan. James, possessive and old-fashioned, had never been told his daughter had lived with Morgan. James Wilde understood the new morality, but not where his daughter was concerned.

"He's invited me to lunch tomorrow," Delia said. "Why would he do that if he knows he's going to sign, anyway?"

"He's testing you," Mary replied confidently. "I can't think of any other reason. Darling, it can't be easy for him, either. I still think he really cared for you. It makes him vulnerable if you direct the picture. Can you see that?"

Delia considered this for a moment, her forehead wrinkled in concentration. Morgan, afraid of her? She shook her head. The thought was laughable. Mary was a hopeless romantic if she thought Morgan had any feelings for an affair that had been dead for six years. And she couldn't picture him vulnerable at all.

"I should go, then?" She didn't want to think about Morgan any more tonight.

Mary nodded her head emphatically. "Definitely. Show him you aren't afraid. You have all the cards, darling. And if he does refuse, we'll cast someone else."

"But it has to be Morgan!" she cried, then stopped, embarrassed by her outburst.

"I know." Mary patted her hand. "You want the picture to be perfect for James."

Delia nodded her head. But did she want Morgan in the film for her father or for herself?

Mary stood, then leaned over to give Delia a quick kiss. "Get to bed soon, all right?"

"I will." There was something in her stepmother's expression that made Delia want to comfort her. She stood up quickly, put her arms around Mary and hugged her tightly.

"I know," she whispered. "I know how much it hurts to watch this happen to James." She hugged her stepmother tightly, trying to control her own emotions.

Mary broke the embrace, wiping her eyes. "I'm so sorry, Delia. It's just that I can't believe—"

"Neither can I—"

"He looks so good. He was so surprised when he opened the door and everyone was here—"

"You've given him everything, Mary." And it was true. Delia gave her stepmother a shaky smile.

As quickly as her stepmother's emotion had burst forth, it was contained again. Mary squeezed Delia's arm. "Don't stay up all night, Delia. You look exhausted."

As Mary slid the glass door open, Delia walked over to the rail of the balcony.

Three months ago Dr. Taylor had found the tumors. James had gone into surgery immediately. She and Mary had thought the worst was over. But afterward they had been told the malignancy had spread. Now it was only a matter of time.

So Delia had moved out of her townhouse and come back to her father's home, and all the while she'd thought about what would make the rest of her father's life as full as possible. And her idea for his final film was born.

She was no stranger to the intricate world of filmmaking. It was part of the legacy James had given her, and she had taken it simply by virtue of being born. That was why she had planned the film as carefully as if she had been executing a battle. From the first call to her godfather, Bob Rosenthal, to finding the perfect script, to the party tonight. She had overseen it all.

And it always came back to her father. James Wilde had been forty-two years old when he met and married her mother, Danielle, a French film actress twenty-one years his junior. Theirs had been a stormy and tempestuous relationship. Delia had learned years later she'd been the reason they'd married. By the time she was five, she had sensed the undercurrents of hostility and tension. When they divorced three years later, she had been relieved.

But she had also been afraid, and guilty. Tall and thin, with her dark hair stick straight, she had been painfully shy as a child. Also, disobedient and temperamental. Her mother had finally decided that James needed to learn what being a father really meant.

Delia had been shipped out to her father's ranch for her eleventh summer. At first, the open land and immense mountains of Wyoming had terrified the child, used to her familiar life in

Paris. Her father, older and more occupied with his career, had not known what to do with the shy little girl.

Mary had helped. She had worked full time at the bank in Jackson Hole until the day James walked in to deposit a huge sum of money, Delia in tow behind him. He had only needed to take one look at Mary. Impulsive as ever, he married her four weeks later.

But Mary was of a temperament totally different from that of Danielle. She fit into their lives as comfortably as if she'd always been there. Understanding the differences that separated Delia from the neighboring children, Mary had arranged for her stepdaughter to take riding lessons at once. Within months, Delia was galloping over the countryside playing cowboys and Indians with the other ranchers' children. The shy child bloomed into a pretty, self-confident adolescent.

And so Delia had grown up in two worlds, shuttled back and forth between her mother's apartment in Paris and her father's sprawling ranch outside Jackson Hole. Until she left for the East Coast and Vassar. Four strenuous years followed, the last two spent abroad in England. Though Delia had vowed not to pursue her father's line of work, she found herself drawn to it. Then Morgan had entered her life and turned it completely around.

She shook her head, impatient with the memories. Despite her father's arguments, she had used her maternal grandmother's last name, not

wanting to use her famous father as a spring-
board to success. Perhaps that was why Morgan's accusation had made her so angry.

*But what he thinks of me really doesn't matter,
anyway.* The only thing that mattered was getting
the film made before James was too weak to
continue.

Passing her father's room, her footsteps muffled in the thick carpet, she stopped before his
door and listened to the quiet house. How many
times in her childhood had she padded down the
hall to her father's room, scared of thunder or
remnants of a nightmare. The monsters underneath the bed had never seemed quite as terrify-
ing when she was wrapped in one of her father's
hugs. James had always welcomed her, soothed
away the myriad hurts of childhood.

Her fingers gently touched the brass doorknob, the metal cool and impersonal under her
fingertips. She touched the door, the gesture
wistful as a small child's.

She couldn't walk in that door, not tonight.
James was battling his own private hell. All she
could give him now was the picture.

Once inside her bedroom, she slipped out of
her evening dress. The black silk hung shape-
lessly against the bathroom door without her
figure to give it form. Delia quickly divested
herself of her sandals, stockings and undercloth-
ing.

After a hot shower and once she was securely
belted into her white terry robe, she stepped out
of the stall. She had left the bathroom door

open, so the mirror was clear. As she headed toward her bedroom, she rubbed her wet hair vigorously with the hood of her robe. But when she caught sight of her reflection in the mirror, she stopped.

Rose Red. The woman who stared back at her had black hair and pale skin. Bright blue eyes fringed with spiky lashes were set in a slim, oval face. Her nose was patrician, an inheritance from her mother's Italian father. Her lips, even without lipstick, were delicately formed and well colored. The top lip had an almost perfect cupid's bow, the bottom full and soft.

Black as ebony, white as ivory, blue as periwinkles, red as a rose—she shook her head to clear out thoughts of a strong, dark man.

MORGAN LAY ON THE BED inside his rented house, listening to the waves rushing up and down the beach. He couldn't sleep.

You handled things badly, letting your emotions get the better of you. But he'd never been able to totally hide his feelings from Delia. She'd managed to open him up more than anyone he'd ever known.

She tore you open once before. And if you do this film, you'll give her a chance to do it again.

There had been a time when he'd thought of building an empire for her. For without an empire to call his own, what right did he have to her?

Delia Wilde. A princess, the press called her. And James Wilde was king.

He'd always felt like her subject.

But you still care. He closed his eyes against the thought.

When she'd left him, he hadn't been angry with her. Things had worked out exactly as he'd expected. What future could there have been for the two of them? A princess and a struggling actor—it had been laughable.

So he'd decided success would be his God, and he'd amassed a fortune. And when he sat back, after all the work was done, he discovered something.

All the riches in the world didn't make him feel any more worthy of her.

So he'd pretended. Pretended it didn't matter they were no longer together. He'd lied to himself so successfully he'd almost begun to believe it. Delia had been the only person who'd slowly peeled away all his protective layers. Simply by loving him. He knew that hadn't been an act.

She hadn't been that experienced.

He'd kept track of her life. It wasn't hard; the press cataloged her every move. He'd seen all her films. Scanned the paper, read about her social life, been blindly jealous of the men who had escorted her to various functions.

Then he received Bob Rosenthal's call. About a very special part, working opposite James Wilde.

As an actor who was known for his good judgment in picking projects, he most certainly would have accepted it.

But knowing Delia would be near her father—he knew he was going to do the film.

But Delia directing it? He hadn't counted on that. An actor was supremely vulnerable during filming; he had to give everything over to the director's vision of the picture.

And the one person he didn't want to be vulnerable in front of was Delia.

Don't let her get to you.

He could never give Delia the upper hand with his emotions. Never again. It hadn't been her fault. She'd been an easy person to open up to.

He shifted his arm so it was over his eyes, blocking out the beginnings of sunrise.

It just hurt too much.

DELIA BELIEVED nothing Morgan could do would unnerve her as much as their encounter on the balcony. But she was wrong.

He answered the door in his swimming trunks, his muscular body bronzed and dripping with water. As he flicked his dark hair out of his eyes with an impatient gesture, she thought he looked like a young Poseidon.

"You're early." His black eyes searched her face as if demanding an answer.

She shrugged her shoulders, trying to still the rapid beating of her heart. Why did this man have to have such a—such a *physical* effect on her? She kept her voice low and steady as she answered.

"You know I hate to be anything but punctual. I called Bob, and he gave me directions to your house. I've never been up this way, and I didn't want to keep you waiting."

He seemed to accept her answer. Stepping back, he ushered her inside.

It was a small beach house, almost a cottage. Totally unpretentious. *Nothing at all like its owner.* A soft smile curved her lips.

"What are you thinking about?"

She felt her features freeze as she carefully tried to school her expression. "Nothing at all. Really." She decided her best course of action was to change the subject. "You must be uncomfortable in that wet suit. I can amuse myself if you want to change into something more comfortable."

The minute she saw the expression on his face, she could have bitten her tongue. Dark brows lifted in disbelief; an amused smile touched the corners of his mouth. "Delia, I can assure you I'm not the slightest bit uneasy—but if you're having a problem..." His voice trailed off suggestively.

Damn him! "Wear whatever you want," she replied coldly, turning away.

She didn't want to look at his body, at such a perfect specimen of the male animal. But knowing the man underneath the hard muscle was devoid of softer emotions, unable to make any commitment in love, helped her. Wasn't that part of the reason she had left him? Delia never wanted to feel that quietly helpless again.

"Shall we go into the dining room?" Morgan asked smoothly, taking her arm before she could say a word.

His dining room turned out to be a small redwood deck with separate levels. Bright tubs of herbs and flowering plants spilled their color and pungent fragrances into the spicy salt air. A hammock swung lazily in the breeze in a far corner. The steps led straight down to white sand and roaring waves.

Delia forgot her previous unease. "How lovely." She let go of Morgan's arm and walked to the edge of the deck. It took her a few seconds before she realized she'd spoken aloud.

"I like it," Morgan replied. She turned back toward him and saw he was watching her, a dark, hard look on his face.

"You spend a lot of time out here," she said, her eyes moving over his deeply tanned body.

He nodded, his gaze never leaving hers. "When I first moved out here, it seemed as if I were living in an endless summer."

"I remember the weather in London." The minute the words were out of her mouth, she regretted them.

His expression changed then, his features altering subtly. "This is nothing like London at all."

She knew he wasn't talking about the weather. The silence lengthened between them. She didn't want to talk about the past.

"Do you own this house?" she asked, hoping to edge the conversation back into more neutral territory.

"I always lease ... with an option to buy."

How like him, Delia thought. The perpetual gypsy. In all the time she had known him, Morgan had never talked much about any family or where he was from. Strange she had lived with him, loved him, yet knew so little about how the boy had shaped the man. Perhaps that was why she'd felt she'd never really understood him.

"Can I help you with lunch?"

He shook his head. "Just sit right here." He led her to a small wooden picnic table with benches. A carafe filled with daisies graced the center. Flatware was wrapped in bright blue napkins, and small ceramic salt and pepper shakers completed the table setting.

Morgan disappeared inside the house while Delia sat down. She crossed her legs, uncrossed them, then stood up and walked nervously over to the edge of the deck.

What kind of man had Morgan become? As she had followed him through his house, she had been unable to tell anything about him from his surroundings. The furnishings were plain; overstuffed chairs and a large couch upholstered in dark blue canvas. Several abstracts hung on the white walls. Delia thought she had seen a Kandinsky. Small bamboo tables were piled high with books and half-read scripts.

Yet there was no warmth—no plants, no photos, no bric-a-brac—none of the things that made the transition from plain house to warm home. She couldn't help but contrast it to the small flat they had shared. It had been cluttered, filled to overflowing with books and playbills. Photos of their vacations had hung in the small hallway. The quilt on their bed had been worn but colorful. She had grown herbs on the windowsill.

Where has his soul gone? Before she could explore this thought further, Morgan appeared on the porch.

"Lunch is served," he announced. He carried a large blue-and-white ceramic bowl in his hands. Setting it down on the table, he returned to the interior of the house.

Delia walked back toward the table, then around it. Familiar smells assaulted her senses as she recognized the green, earthy smell of pesto. It carried her back to other times, to their small kitchen in London. She had loved making this dish for Morgan, though it had been time-consuming. But they had talked and laughed as she crushed each basil leaf with a mortar and pestle, then added garlic and olive oil. Morgan had always boiled the pasta and put the bread to warm.

Her thoughts were broken as he returned with a bottle of white wine and a bowl filled with grated parmesan cheese.

"Sit down." He sounded as if he were giving a stage command. She obeyed automatically.

He sat opposite her and proceeded to dish the pasta out into her bowl. After passing her the cheese, he filled his bowl, then turned his attention to uncorking the wine.

There was something unbearably intimate about eating with Morgan again. Her pesto sauce could have been made of ashes for all the pleasure it gave her.

Morgan poured the wine, then picked up his fork.

They ate in silence. Delia wondered what he was thinking. She remembered the times they had driven down to Italy. Though Morgan had been a dedicated actor, he had also believed in complete vacations to revive the senses. Once he'd found out Italy was one of Delia's favorite countries, he had made it a point to take her there every year.

She remembered long afternoons lying by the ocean, wrapped in his arms. Evenings spent walking, taking in the street life that was such a part of everyday life in Italy. Colors had been brighter, life fuller, their jokes funnier. And all because of the man by her side.

Abruptly, she pushed her plate away.

"Don't you like it?" He seemed genuinely concerned.

"I'm on a diet. I don't eat much pasta anymore." She lied and wished desperately she had never accepted his offer of lunch. Spending this time close to Morgan, yet not close, was beyond endurance. It was too painful to remember what was. And what might have been.

His cool glance assessed her body. "You don't look like you need to diet," he remarked. But he didn't say another word for the remainder of the meal.

When he finished, he picked up both bowls and the larger serving dish and carried them inside.

Delia picked up her wineglass and took a sip, then shifted in her seat to stare out to sea.

I cannot do it. No matter how much James wants him in the picture. She swallowed against the tightness in her throat. *It hurts too much to see him again.*

Morgan returned with another large bowl and proceeded to dish salad onto their plates.

"You can eat this," he assured her. "Nothing fattening for you here." He smiled, the expression bringing sudden warmth to his eyes and making him look younger, less harried, than his thirty-four years. Delia bit her lip, then looked down and picked up her fork.

It was delicious. He certainly hadn't been starving without her. Delia ate quietly, not looking up, not wanting to acknowledge who she was eating with.

When she finally met his eyes, she knew he had been watching her. She felt compelled to say something, no matter how inane.

"Very good dressing," she commented.

"I lifted the recipe from a girl friend. It's the raspberry vinegar that makes it taste so sweet."

A pain she had not thought possible knifed through her chest and took the capacity for breath away. She looked down at the remaining salad on her plate and put her fork down. Images of another woman in Morgan's arms tormented her; beautiful, successful, adept in dealing with him. Everything she was not.

She watched as Morgan cleared away the dishes, then set out a small coffeepot. Pouring a tiny amount of coffee into a bowl, he mixed sugar with it until it created a thick, light brown paste. He spooned a little into one cup, then looked at her.

"Do you still take lots of sugar?"

He remembered. She was ridiculously, childishly, pleased.

"Yes. It smells so good." She indicated the coffeepot in front of him.

"It's my one indulgence. I can't stand American coffee. It's treated with something that makes it bitter. But there's a shop on Rodeo Drive where I buy Italian coffee." He poured the dark, fragrant liquid into both their cups. "It's outrageously expensive, but I have to have it."

The scent of espresso filled the air as Delia lifted the cup to her lips. The coffee-sugar mixture made a slight foam on top. If she closed her eyes, she could easily imagine herself back in Italy with Morgan.

Resolutely, she kept her eyes open. They had finished their meal, and Delia remembered the original purpose of her visit. *He's testing you.* She had to be on her guard.

"Let's sit down by the steps," he said, picking up his coffee and walking to the edge of the deck.

She followed him, admiring the easy grace of his body. Much of the actor's craft had come easily to Morgan. He had a natural physical presence and a relaxed sexuality that could abruptly shift into high intensity whenever the scene demanded it. It had taken Delia years after she had left him before she was able to watch him in a film. But she finally had and realized at the same time that Morgan had developed into a superb actor.

The question that had subconsciously nagged at her all afternoon surfaced with sudden clarity. Could she ever trust him, or was he acting with her again? How could she be sure? And how could she ever work impartially with a man she had once loved so intensely?

As if reading her mind, Morgan seemed to pluck her thoughts out of the air.

"It won't be easy."

"What?" She pretended not to understand, but her hand was shaking.

"Working with you."

They sat on the steps, balancing their cups. Delia was glad she had tied her hair back. The ocean air was blowing briskly, and small strands stung her face.

"You know it's very unusual for a woman director your age to be in charge of a film like this."

Delia stiffened. She knew Morgan too well. Was he moving in for the kill? This sudden about-face couldn't be trusted. But she decided to be honest—partially.

"Yes, it is. I would never have gotten it if it wasn't for my father," she admitted quietly.

"At least you're honest."

She remained silent.

He took a sip of his coffee and set his cup down. "Where did the script come from?"

This was safe ground. "A writing class at UCLA. I knew one of the instructors in a

screenplay-writing class. When he told me about
the script, I arranged to have it mailed to James."

"Who wrote it?"

She smiled. "You'll love this, Morgan. Unconsciously, she slipped into a relaxed manner of
speaking with him. "Charlie is in his sixties and
has loved movies all his life. He used to work in
the university film library, but now he's retired.
He took the class, and his teacher said this script
just came tumbling out of him."

"The script will be shot as is?"

She nodded.

"Do you feel up to it?"

*No, I've never felt more unsure of anything in my
entire life.* "I'm as ready as I'll ever be."

"Are you scared?" Morgan always had a talent for getting straight to the heart of a matter.

Delia thought quickly of her father, to the un-
guarded moments when she had glimpsed the
pain in his face, the acceptance in his eyes. She
remembered the few times she had found Mary
weeping and how her harsh, strangled sobs had
sounded.

That was courage.

"No. Not of the movie."

"What are you scared of?"

She studied his face, taking in his black eyes,
the chiseled facial structure, the strong jaw.

"Sometimes I think—" She stopped, confused, and set her coffee cup down on the deck.
Was it the wine making her more honest, less
afraid? The words slipped out so easily she almost believed she had merely thought them.

"I'm afraid of you."

His expression remained impassive, but she saw something in his eyes, a glimmer of reaction. His voice was soft when he replied.

"Is there another man in your life?"

"No. Only my father."

His arm slipped around her shoulders, his bare chest warm against her side. Delia let his arm remain, strangely comforted by his touch. She knew he was going to kiss her. And she wanted him to.

"There have been times I've missed you." His breath tickled her ear.

"I'm sure." She wanted to remain cool and aloof, but she was melting inside.

"I never stopped wanting you."

She felt sudden tears burn her eyes. *Wanting isn't the same as loving.*

"Why did you leave?"

Of all the questions Morgan could have asked her, it was the last she expected.

Tears filled her eyes. She bent her head and pulled her knees up against her face. Morgan let her sit like that for a long time. He stroked her hair, the back of her neck, her narrow shoulders through the thin cotton of her T-shirt.

Delia felt her emotions surging dangerously out of control. If Morgan had been attractive six years ago, age had given him a more masculine aura. The promise she'd seen in him had been fulfilled. But she suspected he was still the same man underneath.

She lifted her head. "Morgan, if we work together, I don't want to start up our old relationship." His eyes darkened slightly, but she continued. "I want you to be in the film, and so does James. But that's it. Do you understand?"

"No." His answer was barely a whisper before his hand quickly cupped her chin, turning her head toward his.

She pulled away as his lips met hers, then felt his fingers tighten; then his other hand touched her cheek, cupped her face and brought her back around to meet his kiss. It was a deep kiss, long and warm, without reserve. Delia struggled slightly, put her hands against his shoulders and pushed. Her efforts were ineffectual. Morgan took the lead with all the intimate skill she remembered, and soon she felt herself begin to respond, begin not to care.

His lips left hers for an instant, then moved over her cheek to her ear, then her temple, then the tip of her nose and back to her mouth. This time her lips parted willingly as she took in the taste of him, his warmth and scent, the hard feel of his shoulders. She was holding on to him as if by letting go she might spin off the balcony and into the bright hot sky with the force of emotion exploding inside her.

His lips moved down her neck, then to her shoulder. "So sweet," he whispered.

The respite gave her a chance to breathe again. To think. He kissed her shoulder, and she felt his warm, inviting mouth move slowly up her neck. In another instant he would claim her lips again.

"No." With sudden clarity she knew she couldn't continue to let this happen. If she had been afraid to work with Morgan before, she knew it would be impossible if they made love. And that was exactly the direction this meeting was taking.

She pushed at his chest. His grip tightened. "Morgan, *no*." Her voice was low and firm.

He stood up and moved away from her, but his eyes never left her face. She saw an inner fire burn, lighting the black depths of his gaze as he watched her. Waiting. She didn't move until he broke the silence.

"What is it you want, Delia?"

You. "I want you to work on this film." She swallowed nervously, aware of his studying her every movement. "I want our relationship to be as professional as possible. On and off the set."

He sat down a few feet away from her, then leaned back on his elbows, and she tried not to stare at the solid muscles in his chest, the thick black hair. Her eyes moved lower, and she wrenched her gaze away, mortified.

He laughed, totally unashamed of his arousal. "Despite what the press may print, I'm totally human. You know that. Don't you, Delia?"

She kept perfectly still and stared blindly out to sea. In the space of five minutes, everything was totally out of control.

"Delia," Morgan began, his voice low, intimate, a verbal caress. "We're good together. We respect each other. And it isn't as if we're both virgins." When she didn't answer, he continued.

"I don't understand you. A few minutes ago I know you wanted to make love."

She clenched her hands into fists until her nails bit into her palms. He knew her so well. Yet how could he use the word love to describe what had happened? There was none on either side.

Suddenly, she was tired. She stood up before he had a chance to say anything more and walked over to the table where they had eaten. She thought about sitting down again but knew they would only resume the same conversation. Over and over again it seemed they were destined to want different things, feel different ways. If he were a man capable of the tiniest amount of reciprocal feeling for her, Delia knew she would move mountains, make miracles happen for them.

But he wasn't.

"I'm leaving, Morgan." He was standing now, his muscular body almost silhouetted against the bright sun. "Will you be doing the picture or not?"

He approached her, and it took every inch of her willpower not to move away and walk toward the front door of his house.

"Why do you act this way?" His dark eyes assessed her. "You're twenty-eight years old, Delia. Surely you can't be as innocent to the ways of the world as you act." His tone was slightly mocking, as if he enjoyed the thrust of his words. Words designed to hurt.

I want you to love me the way I loved you. "I want to direct this film with a minimum of complications. If you want an affair—" she prayed her voice wouldn't tremble "—then we'll wait until after filming is completed." She watched his reaction.

His dark eyes narrowed, and his face hardened almost imperceptively. "I see. If I run after you like a child, I get the candy stick at the end. Is that it?"

Frustrated, her temper reached boiling point. "Damn you! Why are you acting this way? The script's the best you've had in ages. You'd work beautifully with my father. All the elements are there, but you persist in ignoring them." She took a deep breath. "What the hell do you want?"

"You."

She walked back into the cool, shaded interior of his house. Her steps never faltered as she reached the front door and flung it open.

She was almost to her car when his hand closed over her upper arm. "Delia, wait."

She stopped. She wouldn't make a scene, wouldn't fight him. She knew one thing about Morgan—he wouldn't take her by force. And she certainly wasn't willing anymore.

"I've never felt about any woman the way I feel about you."

She looked up at his face, seeking visual confirmation that he wasn't joking. But he was serious. A long moment passed as she studied the strong planes of his jaw, the determined thrust of his chin. Despite her mental cautiousness, a wild joy began to fill her body, making her want to press herself against him and give up this hateful farce. Over and over in her mind his words played through her consciousness.

I've never felt about any woman the way I feel about you.

She barely heard his next words.

"I've never stopped wanting you."

His words cut deeply, erasing all feeling. She moved stiffly, disengaging his hand like an automaton.

"Delia." He seemed confused.

"Let me go."

"What the hell is the matter with you!"

She began to walk toward her car, digging into her pockets for the keys.

He caught up with her again. "Listen to me. I've never said that to any woman, no matter what you may think."

"I suppose I should be honored."

He let go of her suddenly. "Grow up, Delia." He sounded as if he had to force the words out of his mouth.

"And what?" She smoothly unlocked the door, marveling at the precision of her movements though her hands were trembling. "And sleep with you? And be hurt all over again when you decide to call it off?" She disliked her own vulnerability, but the words wouldn't stop. "No, thanks, Morgan."

"You were the one who walked out on me!" His voice was angry, harsh.

She stopped, confused. He sounded like a man who had been deeply hurt. Could she believe him? Then she remembered. "One of the

Finest Actors in the Western World," *Time* had
christened him. How could she be sure?

"And no one walks out on Morgan Buckmaster. Is that it?" She opened the door and slid
inside. A second later she started the car, then
drove out into the stream of traffic without looking back at him.

Delia drove as far as the next curve on Pacific
Coast Highway, then had to pull over. Her hands
were shaking so badly she could barely grasp the
wheel.

She closed her eyes and leaned back in the
seat. Her body was so tense it hurt. After so
many years, she was still angry with Morgan.
How could she possibly work with him, feeling
the way she did? It was impossible.

But the decision had already been made. Morgan wouldn't agree to do the film after the way
she had treated him. She'd have to start con-
sidering other actors for the role. James would
be disappointed.

James. She opened her eyes and looked out
over the ocean, trying to derive a sense of calm
from the pounding waves. How could she have
done this to her father?

And how would she explain this to him? He
had no idea of her previous relationship with
Morgan. He would never understand. And his
heart was set on working with Morgan.

I cannot deal with any of this. She covered her
ears as if to ward off her thoughts. After a few
minutes Delia started the car and eased it out
into traffic again.

When she got home, Mary and James were

out on the balcony. Delia avoided both of them on the way to her room. Once inside, she threw herself down on her bed and stared at the ceiling.

How would she ever tell James? She turned over and buried her face in her pillow. The childish gesture was comforting.

Maybe someone else should direct the picture. The idea came to her swiftly, but she rejected it immediately. She'd be damned if she'd let Morgan take this away from her after she'd come this far!

Her afternoon had been exhausting. *Just ten minutes.* She rolled over and shut her eyes.

It seemed like only minutes later that Mary was shaking her gently awake. "Delia, Morgan's on the phone. He wants to speak to you."

So he can gloat and tell me he's refusing to sign. She felt dull and tired as she walked into the hall and picked up the phone.

"Hello, Morgan."

"Hello, Delia. I called to tell you that while I still don't approve of the idea of your directing, I'll take the part." He paused. She waited for him to speak again, knowing he wouldn't be able to resist getting in the last word after their earlier fight.

"And Delia, I'm only doing this because I want to work with James Wilde."

She sat down suddenly, and it seemed as if all the air left her lungs. Had she heard him correctly? She was so lost in pleasure that she had to concentrate to hear the rest of what he was saying.

"One slip and I'll insist on hiring a real director, so you'd better damn well know what you're doing. Am I making myself perfectly clear? I'll put you through hell on the set if I think you're not doing your job."

"Thank you, Morgan. All clear. I understand, and I'll see you on the set." She hung up before he could say another word.

James! With a laugh of pure pleasure, Delia ran to find her father.

Chapter Three

The stable smelled of straw and liniment as Delia walked past the row of box stalls. An early-morning ride was just the thing to calm her before Morgan arrived later today. She was still as nervous with him as a virgin approaching the bridal bed.

They'd spent six weeks in Los Angeles, shooting interiors. And in all that time Morgan still hadn't come close to respecting her. He did his job, but he'd made it painfully clear to her he was working with James, not with her. And Delia had felt she was walking on eggs, always careful to avoid him as much as possible. Which wasn't much.

She'd managed to shoot extra footage of her father, especially close-ups. So far the picture seemed to have invigorated James, and he'd put all his energy into the project.

All exteriors would be shot at the ranch. Delia was thankful the early-May weather was mild, with bright, clear sunshine. So far, everything was running exactly on schedule, and she hadn't gone over budget.

I just can't stand the thought of another six weeks of Morgan acting like a prima donna. Funny how he was being so temperamental toward her when he'd abhorred that type of behavior back in London.

He must still hate me for leaving, she thought grimly. *But he pushed me to it.*

Some of the horses whickered gently, and she was gently brought out of her memories. A few stamped their hooves and swished their tails. She paused by one stall, larger than the rest, and peeked inside. Falstaff, her father's champion quarter horse, stood solidly inside, his chestnut coat gleaming faintly in the early-morning light. A brilliant white blaze illuminated his intelligent face. He moved gracefully over to the edge of his stall so that Delia could scratch behind his ears.

She petted him as if he were a small child, delighting in the feel of smooth hair over hard muscle. Scrambling up and hooking her leg over the stall door, she hopped inside and ran her hands over his massive withers, his hindquarters. Falstaff snorted with pleasure.

"What a good boy you are," she said, falling into the habit they all shared of talking to the horses without even realizing it. "I'm taking Cinderina for a ride today, or I'd take you. But you don't really like anyone but James on your back, do you?" She reached into the pocket of her denim jacket and produced a lump of sugar.

Falstaff had a notorious sweet tooth. She held it out to him, her palm flat, and almost laughed at the sensation of his soft lips as they tickled quickly over her palm in search of the sweet. She patted him again.

"You're waiting for James, aren't you?" The horse watched her silently, understanding seeming to radiate from liquid brown eyes. "He's not feeling well these days, Falstaff, but I promise you he'll ride you in the film." With this last message she opened the stall door and exited properly.

Within fifteen minutes she had bridled and saddled Cinderina and was leading her out onto the cement floor of the stable. Horse and rider walked silently through the rows of stalls until they were at the east exit, facing the rising sun. And freedom.

She was swinging up into the saddle when she heard a familiar voice.

"Cordelia Wilde, what's bothering you this early in the morning?" Tom Donahue, stable manager, short and wiry as a bantam rooster, came sauntering out into the cool morning air.

She smiled. She should have known better than to try to avoid Tom. And no one ever fooled him. Working with horses the way he did, the smallest nuance of human behavior couldn't escape his practiced eye, and he'd probably been watching her from the moment she stepped into the stable yard. James had brought him back from Ireland. The two men had met at the Dublin races and started to argue over James's buying a particular horse. A strong friendship had developed, and Tom had agreed to come back to Wyoming and work on James's ranch. The bond between the two men had extended to include the entire family.

"I just thought I'd take a ride, that's all," she replied, imitating his brogue, throwing the gauntlet back at him. She loved Tom dearly.

"Don't lie to this one." A short, stubby finger jabbed at his chest. "It's worried you are about something, and I mean to find out!"

She sat back in the saddle and laughed. Some of the tension left her chest. Relieved now that she hadn't been able to escape him, she swung down and led Cinderina over to where Tom stood, his short legs slightly bowed.

"It's James. It's the film. Morgan Buckmaster arrives today. Oh, Tom—I'm just so scared. It never stops." Once this admission was out, the words began to tumble, one jumping over the other. "I've never done anything like this before, and I'm not quite sure that I can finish it— and if I fail James now, I'll never be able to forgive myself. He wants this film so badly, and I want people to remember him as—"

"Whoa, darling." Tom held up his hand. "I'll saddle Falstaff and meet you here in a minute. We'll take them down by the lake and have a good talk."

He returned with the big, gentle horse within minutes as promised, and the two of them set off.

The sun was just rising, and tall meadow grass

rippled in the slight breeze. The air was thin and pure, a total contrast to the brown smog in Los Angeles. They let the horses move slowly, content to simply give them their heads.

Delia breathed deeply of the cool, tangy air. She loved this time of the morning. As a child, she had always been an early riser, had been out at the stables before breakfast, tagging behind Tom or her father. Life on the ranch had a simple, primitive rhythm she missed when she was in Los Angeles. Here you knew where you were, what you did, where the day led. It was simply home.

After fifteen minutes, Tom tightened his reins and suggested they head toward the lake. Delia gathered her reins and gave Cinderina a gentle squeeze with her legs. The bay mare responded at once, breaking into a trot and then a rolling canter. She fell into the horse's rhythm easily. Tears burned her eyes as the wind rushed up to meet her face, but she kept her eyes open and crouched low over the mare's back.

She was galloping now; the relentless thud of the mare's hooves was fast and steady. Delia urged her on, conscious of Tom beside her, conscious of the loudness of Falstaff's hooves. She ran the mare until they were almost a quarter of a mile away from the lake, then began to pull on the reins, making the animal slow.

They dismounted and walked the rest of the way, the horses snorting and wheezing, flecks of foam on their necks and withers. The lake was one of Delia's favorite places on the ranch property. Morainal, carved out of the ground by a glacier during the same ice age that had created the mountains surrounding the valley, it shimmered, cool and serene in the early-morning light.

"Falstaff isn't even tired yet. That one—" Tom jerked his head toward Cinderina "—needs someone to ride her on a regular basis." He cleared his throat. "It's glad I am you're back on the ranch where you belong."

Delia felt quick tears sting her eyes, and she directed her gaze toward the lake, away from Tom as she blinked them away. A damselfly danced over the surface of the water, a silver-green blur. As quickly as she saw it, the insect darted away.

"How's the old man?" Tom asked gruffly. He was the only one, other than herself, Mary and Dr. Johnson, the local physician, who knew of James's condition.

"The same. He's perked up because of the film. I hope he'll make it through all the exteriors—I've planned his scenes so they're the first we shoot."

Tom nodded. He didn't reply, so she knew he wanted her to go on.

"I want this film to be good, Tom. I don't give a damn about my own career at this point. I just want it to be good for him—" As tears clogged her throat, she stopped talking and stared blindly at the lake.

Tom was silent, waiting for her to continue.

When she spoke again, her voice shook. "I

just can't believe he's going to die. He seems so cheerful some mornings, I play a game with myself and pretend everything's all right. But if I look in his eyes or catch him at a tired moment, it all comes back, and I know it's true."

"The man will be missed, that's a certainty."

Delia reached down and picked up a handful of wild grass, crumbling it in her hand. "And the worst thing is, I'm still scared to death of all this! I've never done anything this big before, and I want it to be good so badly I can taste it!"

"Cordelia, do you remember the time I taught you to jump?"

Tom's question caught her completely off guard, and memories came flooding back. He had found her in the stable crying one evening after turning down an invitation to a trail ride. Tom had talked with her and had figured out the reason quickly. Delia didn't know how to jump, and she was terrified of the wilder parts of the country they'd be riding through.

Tom had set to work at once, building jumps in the west corral. He had handpicked My Sweetheart, a rust-colored mare who loved to jump but had a smooth gait and a steady heart. Delia had been panic-stricken at the first fence, but she had hung on as My Sweetheart cleared first one, then another. Tom had sat on the rails by the side, cheering relentlessly. She had hated him for a short time as he forced her to face the dreaded fence again and again. But in the end she had learned. And she never forgot the day she jumped and her fear was replaced by a wild joy. Tom had known then and had told her father. They had all gone out to dinner in Jackson Hole and to a movie afterward. Delia's choice.

And Tom knew this feeling was exactly the same.

"Cordelia, the fear never goes completely away. It just moves on to different things. But if you didn't dare, if you didn't at least try—" His words hung in the clear morning air.

"I know you're right, Tom, but—"

"What does it take to direct one of these films?" he asked bluntly.

Delia sighed. "You have to be on top of everything, what everyone's doing. Their safety is in your hands. The actor's performances are brought out by whatever I can give them to work with. I pick the order we shoot scenes—" She started to laugh. "Oh, what the hell, I'm in charge of the whole damn thing!"

Tom smiled, and his skin creased, like fine old leather. "You can be pretty bossy when you mean to be, miss. I don't understand what your problem is. Sure, all these people have to know it's your first time for a big show like this one."

She could almost hear the words Morgan had blurted out over the phone so long ago in Malibu. An image of him, clear and strong, flashed through her mind with sudden clarity. "Morgan," she murmured unconsciously.

"Morgan, is it? You're worried about the famous Mr. Buckmaster?"

Delia felt her face grow warm and turned her

head away. "He took the news about my direct-ing badly," she admitted.

"Cordelia, girl, the man probably doesn't even know how to sit a horse. He has his fears like anyone else. Don't you understand that?"

She shook her head. Not Morgan. She thought of him as the devil himself, scared of no one, nothing.

"Don't shake your head at me. I know people. I'll take care of this man if he gives you any trouble."

The image of Tom up against Morgan was so amusing Delia bit her lip to keep from smiling. Dear Tom.

"I'll try," she finally admitted. "I'll get this film done one way or another."

When they returned to the stable, Tom of-fered to take care of the mare.

"You look tired, Cordelia. Let me rub down Cinderina and you get inside and let Mary put something in your stomach."

She accepted gratefully, then set off for the farmhouse at a steady lope.

She slammed open the back door and gave Mary a hug.

"It's going to be all right, Mary. I talked to Tom and—"

"Delia." Mary interrupted her enthusiasm with a warning look in her steady brown eyes. "We have guests in the breakfast room. Why don't you go in and say hello?"

Delia froze. She mouthed the word Morgan. Mary nodded.

"Now go in and join them. I'll be there with the waffles in a minute."

"Can I help you?" Delia wanted to postpone the inevitable.

Mary gave her a slight nudge. "Your father is with them, and he had a bad night," she whispered. "I think he's getting tired." Her eyes pleaded with Delia.

Without another word she walked out into the breakfast room to face Morgan.

THE BREAKFAST NOOK was cheery and comfortable, a favorite spot inside the ranch house. But Delia barely took in the cheerful blue-and-white decor as her eyes settled on Morgan and the young woman sitting next to him.

Belinda Peters had been selected over hundreds of actresses for the role of James's daughter. Her romance with Morgan was one of the chief conflicts in the script. Looking at her, Delia had to admit she was perfect for the part of Mary Anne, the rancher's daughter. Her blond hair, shot through with streaks of purest gold, was almost white. Her blue eyes were set in a face composed of startlingly classic features. She looked like a young Grace Kelly. And she was the perfect foil for Morgan's dark looks.

They sat closely together, both dressed for traveling, Morgan in a lightweight suit, Belinda in a feminine skirt and jacket with a ruffly silk blouse underneath. Delia was suddenly aware of her jeans and sweatshirt, and that she smelled of horse.

She bent and kissed her father. "Hello, Dad." He did look tired. "Tom and I went riding this morning. I took Cinderina, and Tom took Falstaff." She noticed the regretful look on her father's face and could have immediately bitten her tongue. James had always loved to ride, but now he had to confine himself to more sedate activities.

But his spirit surprised her. "Did you give the old reprobate some sugar?"

She grinned. "He would have nosed my pocket until he got some; you know that." She turned to include Morgan and Belinda, her equilibrium returning. "Hello, Belinda, Morgan. I hope you both had a good flight."

Belinda nodded, then spoke. Her voice was low and rich, and Delia remembered she had classical training.

"One of your men met us at the airport. I really appreciated that, because I don't think we could have found this place otherwise." She smiled at Delia, her features perfect and glowing.

At that moment, Mary came in with a tray of waffles and a pitcher of heated syrup. A silence descended as everyone began to dish out food.

"I'm going to take off my boots," Delia announced to no one in particular, then exited gracefully.

She reached her room, surprised to find her hands trembling. *From seeing Morgan?* she asked herself. No. *From seeing him with Belinda? Ah, now we're getting close.* Even after weeks of filming in Los Angeles, she still wasn't sure how close they were. Their love scenes had certainly been hot, but all of Morgan's love scenes were. She'd closed her eyes so many times in the privacy of darkened theaters, unable to see him with another woman even on-screen.

So what's it to you? You don't care anymore. She chose to ignore her feelings as she ran a comb through her wind-tangled hair and pulled it back off her face with a band. She wiped a damp washcloth over her dusty face and put on some lip gloss. Changing into a light blue blouse, she took one last look in the mirror and returned to the breakfast table.

They were all still there, but Tom had joined them. His plate was piled high with waffles, and Mary was pouring him another cup of coffee. Delia caught the tail end of his conversation as she entered the room.

"Cordelia tells me all of you can ride, but we don't want any accidents on this film so if any of you need lessons, I'm willing to coach you in the west corral any morning you wish." He looked up at her, and she sent him her silent, heartfelt message. *Bless you, Tom.*

Belinda glanced up from her poached egg and slice of melon. "I'd like that very much, Mr. Donahue. I'm going to need help with that chase scene."

"Oh, but we'll be bringing in a stunt woman for you," Delia interrupted.

"But when I grab her reins at the end of the scene," Morgan said, making her jump, "it can't be a double then, because we go right into dialogue." His expression seemed to convey the silent message *See, once again you don't know what you're doing.*

She controlled her temper with difficulty. "You're right, of course, Mr. Buckmaster." She could tell by the tightening of his mouth that he didn't like the way she addressed him. "But I was referring to the beginning and middle of the chase, and I'm definitely going to use doubles for both of you at that time."

"I see." He stabbed his waffle with his fork, and Delia had the distinct impression that it was her body he wished was on his plate. She looked away.

Belinda glanced at her, and it was evident from the expression in her clear blue eyes that she sensed the tension in the air.

Tom finished his waffles and pushed back his chair. "James, I'd like you to see the Arabian stallion I talked with you about. I'm sure someone slipped him into that last shipment of quarter horses. He's a mean one—as hot-tempered as the devil himself. But once I gentle him he'll be good to the mares, I can assure you."

Delia glanced down at her plate and concentrated on cutting her waffle. Frank talk at the table about the horses was nothing new, but with Morgan here, it made her uneasy. She looked at her father.

His deep blue eyes were sparked with interest. "Mary, we'll be out by the barn." The two older men got up and began to walk outside. Delia noticed that Tom stayed close to her father's side without ever appearing to do so.

Mary began to clear the table, and Belinda offered to help. Delia realized she and Morgan would be the only two people left, so she started to get up.

"Delia, stay." The softness in his voice took her by surprise. "You've barely started to eat. Don't make me responsible for your skipping breakfast."

She couldn't let him know how he affected her. Not if she was ever going to continue directing him in a film. "It isn't you," she said hastily, then took a long swallow of milk. "I want to go out to the barn and get a look at the new stallion."

"Then you won't mind if I come along?"

He had trapped her. Her eyes met his for just an instant. *Touché*, she thought, with grudging admiration. She could hear Mary and Belinda from the kitchen, engaged in animated conversation.

"Belinda?" She nodded her head in their direction.

"She isn't as horse crazy as you are." The words seemed derogatory.

Stung, she got up. "I'll meet you at the barn." Once inside her room, she pulled on her boots. Returning to the breakfast room, she saw him still standing there, waiting. She walked out the front door. Delia could hear his firm steps close behind her, but she didn't care. She hoped he'd fall off and break his neck during the chase scene.

When she reached the corral, she propped her elbows on the weathered gray wood and settled her chin against her arms. Morgan walked up beside her.

"Why are you always so damn touchy?"

She didn't even favor him with a look. "Touchy? I don't know what you mean."

They were interrupted by shouts of admiration as a black stallion exploded into the paddock, two thousand pounds of compressed energy. He charged around the enclosure, swerving as he approached the fence. The stallion held his powerful body at a proud angle, head erect, nostrils flaring.

Delia could see her father at the other end of the corral, surrounded by several of the hired hands. With sudden clarity, she realized that *this* was where he belonged, not in front of a camera. And she knew she was doing the best thing she possibly could by blending his two worlds.

The stallion stopped moving and pawed the ground with delicate, impatient hooves. His loud whinny broke the stillness of the air. An Arabian, he was streamlined and patrician, with a fiery temperament.

Tom joined them at the rail. He patted Delia affectionately on her shoulder. "Come on, miss. You're the one who always names them. Give this wild one a title worthy of all that fire!" He grinned and took off his hat, wiping his face with his shirt sleeve. "Your father is absolutely delighted. I haven't seen him look so good since—" He stopped, aware of Morgan behind him. "Give us a name, Cordelia."

She frowned. "Black as sin, wild as the wind—"

She played with the words as they rolled off her tongue. Suddenly, she laughed. "We have to have a literary allusion, for James. How about Mephistopheles?"

"Lucifer?" Morgan suggested, joining in the fun.

"Satan?" Delia replied, then turned to watch the stallion again.

"He looks like he comes from the underworld," Morgan remarked. His sentence fired Delia's imagination.

"Hades!" she shouted, turning to Tom. "Hades, king of the underworld!"

"Hades it is," Tom said, giving her a small mock bow and walking around the corral until he reached her father. A moment later, James gave Delia the thumbs-up sign.

"Hades it is," Morgan repeated. He leaned on the fence, inches away from her. "You know, now that I'm finally here, I can understand why you missed it so much. As Belinda and I were driven in, all I could see was mountains and sky as far as I looked. London must have been awfully confining."

"At times. At times it was—" She stopped herself before the words slipped out. At times it had been the most exciting place on earth, but only because of Morgan.

"At times?" He urged her gently.

"At times it was very pleasant." *Pleasant*, she thought with disgust. Such a tame word to describe what she and Morgan had shared.

He was watching her now, like a hawk with a

mouse. "Your stepmother prepared the guest house for Belinda and me."

Delia felt as if all the air were being slowly squeezed out of her lungs. Her throat closed painfully as she pictured Belinda's fairness against Morgan's dark, virile body, limbs entwined. It wasn't possible that anything could hurt her so much. But this image did.

"I'll be sleeping in the main bedroom," he continued, "but Belinda said she'd take the smaller bedroom off the kitchen." When she didn't reply, he said, "We're not sleeping together, despite what you may think." And without another word he turned and walked away.

Delia didn't look back, didn't watch as he went back toward the ranch house. She heard the kitchen door shut but kept her eyes on the animal in the corral. The long black mane and tail fluttered in the spring breeze; the obsidian eyes flashed.

"I should have named you Morgan," she said to no one in particular, then began to walk around the fence to her father.

THAT WAS THE most adolescent thing you've done since filming began, Morgan thought as he headed back toward the guest house to unpack. He'd been friends with Belinda Peters for years, ever since they'd worked together in London on a play. She'd been in a crowd scene, but her terrified vulnerability had made him notice her. He'd teased her, made her relax and put the job in perspective.

But he hadn't even thought of how beautiful she was, not when Delia had been home at their flat waiting for him.

It was unsettling, being at the ranch. She'd told him about it so many times, made him laugh over all the funny stories about her years growing up, running free. It had sounded like the ideal childhood.

Of course, at the time he'd had no idea who her father was.

Seeing it now brought back so many deeply emotional memories. The times they'd walked around London, neither of them with a penny in their pockets, and woven dreams, confided in each other, spoken from theirs hearts. He could still remember how fragile she'd seemed to him, how proud he'd been to have her hand tucked into his jacket pocket, their fingers entwined.

It had been the beginning of his emotional awakening.

Once inside the guest house, he walked inside the bedroom Mary had given him. Trying to take his mind off Delia, he began to unpack his clothes.

Seeing her here had been so different from seeing her at James's birthday party in Malibu. When she'd burst in the door in her jeans and sweatshirt, looking gloriously alive and earthy, he'd had a quick glimpse of the woman he'd known in London.

She was reserved around him. But he could hardly blame her; he'd acted like a spoiled idiot the entire time they'd been on the set. Looking to James to confirm what she'd just said. Asking sarcastic questions. Giving her pained looks that told her he knew what he was doing, that he didn't need her to spoon-feed him his interpretation of the role.

Yet he knew she was doing a damned good job. She had that way of getting people to trust her and open up. She created an atmosphere of safety on the set, so essential to creativity. He knew Belinda was doing her best work. James certainly was. And, strangely enough, he knew he was reaching deeper than he ever had before.

He would have joyfully taken what she gave him from any other director. But it was so difficult from Delia.

His unpacking finished, he lay down on the bed and closed his eyes. He couldn't relax, even after the flight and the drive to the ranch. He kept seeing Delia the way she'd looked in the breakfast room before she'd glanced at him.

I'm doing a good job of unnerving her. But somehow it wasn't giving him any satisfaction.

The attraction he still had for her seemed constantly in danger of boiling over. He'd been keeping a tight lid on his feelings—that was all he needed, Delia's realizing he still cared.

Everything in his life, from the moment she'd left him, had been done with her in mind.

He deliberately blanked his mind and tried to think of nothing. An image of Hades, the stallion, formed. He smiled grimly.

What had Tom said? He was shipped in and

thrown in with the other horses because he was such a brute.

You're the same way—shipped in and trying to survive among the real thoroughbreds. He felt as if he didn't quite fit in. Everyone was so easy with each other. Even Belinda—the way she'd helped Mary clear the breakfast table this morning.

But he still felt like an outsider among Delia and her family.

He took a deep breath and tried to relax. Shooting started tomorrow morning, and he needed the rest.

His role off-camera promised to be the most demanding part he'd ever played.

Chapter Four

"Cut!"

Delia bit her lip and tried to control her rapidly escalating temper. Morgan was already creating problems. She motioned him over to her with an impatient flick of her hand.

His walk was smooth and assured. Any other actor might have looked anxious. Not Morgan. Was it her imagination, or was he enjoying the entire incident in a perverse way?

Before she could think further, he was standing next to her. She looked up into his dark eyes and tried to read his expression. His face was smooth and blank. He obviously didn't want her to know what he was feeling.

She clenched her hands into fists. "Dan," she said, turning to her cameraman, "tell everyone to take a break. Morgan and I will be back in fifteen minutes."

Without waiting for an answer, she started to walk away from the tangle of people and equipment, cameras and microphones. The entire setup looked incongruous against the immense

Wyoming sky. The mountains rose in the distance, seven thousand feet above the valley floor. Like blue-gray pyramids, they were a tangible presence, solid and eternal. She knew that at the summit there were eternal snows, and the unceasing winds buffeted the granite faces relentlessly. And Delia felt the coldness of the snow within her heart and knew what it was to be buffeted every which way.

Why was Morgan doing this to her? She felt a sudden urge to just keep walking, to divorce herself from the entire project. But she couldn't.

They were twenty feet away before she directed her first question to Morgan.

"Would you mind explaining to me just what you were doing out there?"

He seemed amused. "Just playing my part, ma'am," he drawled in his best western accent.

"Come off it, Morgan." Though she felt as if her stomach were on a roller coaster, Delia knew she had to stand up to him again. Unless she did, there would be continued confrontations between them.

He waited for her to continue, one dark brow raised.

She sighed. "The way you were delivering your dialogue—the emphasis you gave the last scene. It wasn't the way we discussed it the other day."

The change in him was startling, and Delia knew he was angry. "Are you saying that I don't know how to do my job?" he asked softly. But there was just a hint of steel in his voice.

"No, that's not what I'm saying at all," she snapped, irritated. They were wasting valuable time. "The only thing I want you to do is run through the scene once the way I explained it to you." When he didn't answer, she continued. "You're meeting Mary Anne—Belinda—for the first time. You know she's the daughter of the rancher you'll eventually have to fight. But there's a tremendous sexual attraction between the two of you, and I don't think you'd be all that hostile immediately. Do you understand?" She studied his face, trying to find a clue in his black eyes as to how he was feeling.

He smiled, but it didn't reach his eyes. "I've been told, at times, that I'm *very* hostile when all I've thought I was trying to do was convince a particular woman of how sexually attracted I am to her." The look in his eyes left the identity of this particular woman in no question.

Delia averted her gaze and fixed it on the crew in the distance. She hated herself for the telltale blush she could feel burning her cheeks. How had she ever gotten herself into this situation? But there was too much at stake now.

"Morgan, I don't care how attracted you are to *anyone*." *Especially me.* But her thoughts didn't quite ring true. She glared up at him. "We're going to walk back to the set, and you're going to run through that scene the way I want you to. Is that absolutely clear?"

"And if I want to try it another way?"

She pushed a strand of hair out of her face with an impatient gesture. "I'm not a monster, damn it! I'll listen to you, and if I think it might work, you can do whatever you want! But I want the scene on film my way first! Is that clear?''

"Perfectly." His response was clipped, frigid.

"Thank you." She spun away from him on the heel of her cowboy boot and began to walk rapidly back to the set.

The rest of the day was one long disaster. Morgan did everything she requested. But it seemed as if some inner light had been extinguished inside him. He didn't project, he didn't charm, he didn't reach through and make love to the camera. Belinda was patient through take after take, but Delia could see the actress was beginning to tire.

The sky was slowly darkening when Dan tapped her on the shoulder. "I think we'd better wrap it up for the day. We're not going to get anything else done."

Delia nodded, then bent her head so the older man couldn't see the tears starting in her eyes. *Toughen up. Fast.*

Blinking the dampness away, she faced him. "Thanks, Dan. You did a good job today."

Dan took off his cap and scratched the fringe of white hair around his ears. "I don't know what happened to Morgan, but whatever he has left him about two this afternoon."

As if I didn't know. "Yes, I saw it. But we have to remember that actors get tired, too. It must not be one of his better days." Delia signaled to the crew that they were done for the day, then made a conscious effort to walk toward Belinda.

The actress looked even more fragile today. Her prairie skirt was dusty, her white blouse damp with perspiration, and her makeup was just beginning to run. As Delia approached her, she looked up in alarm.

"I'm sorry," she blurted out as Delia came up beside her.

"Don't be. It wasn't anyone's fault." At the look of relief in her blue eyes, Delia warmed to her task. "Everyone has their off days, even Morgan." Though her instincts told her Morgan knew exactly what kind of game he was playing, in that instant with Belinda, Delia decided to give him the benefit of the doubt. He obviously didn't like working under her direction. But today she could afford to be generous.

She touched Belinda's arm gently. "Don't be late for supper. Mary's making fried chicken, and I can tell you from past experience there won't be any leftovers." She grinned. "You were terrific. It's difficult doing the same lines over and over and still try to inject life into them."

Belinda looked amazed. "I—it's—thank you."

"You take direction well."

"Thank you!" Now she looked more flustered than before. Picking up the hem of her skirt so she could walk more easily, Belinda fell into step behind Delia. "Thanks for being so understanding. It's been kind of hectic. Coming all the way out here, setting up and all." She flashed Delia a smile, her teeth perfect and white against her creamy complexion.

Delia sighed. She had seen enough through the lens to know that Belinda photographed like a goddess. Morgan looked his usual forbidding self. It had been an inspired job of casting; they were perfect foils for each other, her fairness against his darkness. If only Morgan would shape up and stop acting like a child!

As if reading Delia's mind, Belinda spoke. "It's curious about Morgan, isn't it?"

Delia made no comment, and the young woman continued, unaware of the tension just beneath the surface.

"I mean, his work today. Usually he's the one who pulls the rest of us up."

"You've worked with him before?" Delia was surprised by this bit of news.

Belinda nodded. "It was a play in London—his first leading role. I was in the crowd scene, but all of us that could stayed for Morgan's rehearsals." Her blue eyes sparkled with the intensity of her memories. "He was like a—like some kind of god to us then. All the boys wanted to be like Morgan. And the girls—well . . ."

She let the rest of her sentence trail off. Delia had stopped listening. Memories rushed back despite her wish to keep them at bay. She could see Morgan's face, more boyish and relaxed, more *vulnerable*, as he bounded up the stairs to their flat and caught her in a bear hug. He had been talking so quickly she'd had trouble catching the words. But at last he had told her about the play, about the particular part. She had listened, enraptured, as she always had. And she had gone to see every single performance except the first. Bad luck for the actor, Morgan had reminded her. She had been so proud of him, and they had been so happy together.

"Wait and see what happens tomorrow. Will we start with the same scenes, do you think?" Belinda's voice, clear and soft, startled her back to full consciousness.

"Yes. Yes, I think so." They were close to the ranch house now, and Delia could make out the individual horses in the paddock against the twilight sky.

"I love that stallion. He's a beauty. But I'd be afraid to ride him." Belinda shivered and pulled her shawl closer around her.

"I may try this weekend, depending on what Tom says." Delia's gaze strayed to the proud equine head, nostrils flaring. The Arabian broke into a floating trot, his delicate hooves barely seeming to touch ground. He was so incredibly spirited, so beautiful. She noticed Tom leaning against the railing and turned toward Belinda.

"I'm going to talk to Tom just a minute before dinner, but you go on in."

"Thanks, Delia." Belinda veered to the right and started toward the house.

When Delia reached the rail, she didn't say anything. Tom's eyes were fastened on Hades, watching the way the stallion switched strides, the way he came close to the paddock fence and no closer. Delia knew he was trying to figure out the best way to gentle the animal.

"What do you think?" she asked softly.

He grinned, slowly, the weather-beaten lines on his face deepening. "I'm thinking that devil is going to be quite a handful—but I like them that way!" His light blue eyes gleamed with admiration as he watched the animal. Its hooves sent up puffs of dust as it cantered. The long black mane and tail streamed out behind as powerful muscles bunched and unbunched beneath the midnight coat.

Delia tried for just the right amount of nonchalance. "What's the best way of taming an animal like that?"

"This one?" Tom took a cigarette out of his pocket and lit it. The tip glowed red against the deep blue sky as he took a drag. "First, you watch them for a while, just to see if they have any unusual habits. This one—" he cocked his head toward the stallion "—he's a restless sort. I'll be needing a lot of patience. I might just stand here awhile and let him get used to me. We're both sizing each other up, you see."

"Yes, but—" Now Delia couldn't keep the tiniest thread of impatience out of her voice. "What about when you know the animal pretty well, or you think you do, and they still give you unexpected trouble?"

Tom narrowed his eyes. "Then for sure I'd check him and make sure he was feeling all right, make sure he was healthy and rested. But if it's not health, then you have to get to work and make the animal come to you."

"But what do you do?"

"With this one? I'll start tomorrow by going

to his stall and offering him a bit of sugar in my hand. If he takes it, then we can go on. If not, I'll leave it on the rail. The important thing, Delia darling, is that the animal has to come to expect good things when you're around. Otherwise, training is always more difficult."

"But what if you don't have too much time and you need to see results?"

Tom frowned. "I could throw a saddle on that black brute's back right now, and I could ride him if I wanted to." He paused, looking at her as if seeing her for the first time. "But I won't. I've seen it done too many times, and it destroys whatever spirit the animal has. You think you win the prize, but you get nothing in the end. Do you understand?"

"I think so." She hunched her shoulders forward and rested her chin on her hands.

Delia felt Tom place his palm on her head and gently ruffle her hair. "Mind you, I'm not suggesting you give Morgan sugar lumps. But then a man is a different animal altogether."

"You always know, don't you?"

He smiled, a gentle smile that creased his weather-beaten face even further. "I asked Dan before he went inside. He told me you and Morgan had a little talk and the rest of the afternoon was wasted. It's not that hard to figure you out."

"If Morgan were a horse— What I mean is—"

"What you mean is, how the devil are you going to get the man to obey you and respect your direction."

"That's it exactly."

Tom rubbed his chin and continued to watch the stallion. The animal was slowing down; the trot had become a walk. "Darling, I'd have a talk with him after dinner. With a full stomach and some good company he may be able to see reason."

The stallion was still now, the only movement the rippling of its mane and tail in the gentle evening breeze.

"Does he know about James?"

"No," Delia admitted. "I don't want anyone to know. I don't want—" Her throat started to tighten, but she pushed past it. "I don't want anyone to pity him or change whatever they're doing! I want him to have this last picture. Just the way it's always been."

"I know." Tom started to say something else, then stopped. Delia watched as he reached into his pocket and took out a lump of sugar. Without saying a word, he took her hand and placed the lump in her palm.

Delia looked up and saw that the stallion was watching them. His ears were pricked forward, his nostrils flared as he took in their scent.

Slowly, ever so slowly, she reached out her hand as far as she could over the fence, the sugar held flat in her palm. She didn't say a word, didn't move a muscle. Tom stood silently beside her.

The stallion began to approach, and as it did, she watched its eyes. Big and black, they registered a certain amount of fear, then curiosity. The stallion stopped. Its nostrils flared again, and

Delia knew he smelled the sugar. Her hand wavered slightly. The lump was growing sticky in her palm.

She concentrated all her attention on the stallion, and as if in answer to her unspoken thoughts, the large animal began to walk slowly toward them.

Delia barely breathed, holding her stomach tightly in case a single movement betrayed her. Still the stallion came nearer, nearer; then suddenly she felt velvet lips move over her palm and take the sugar.

Daring further, she reached up and patted the silken neck. The stallion wheeled and trotted to the center of the paddock.

Tom's expression was proud. "You're the first! You see what I mean! You help them sense you're not going to hurt them, and they respond." He gave her a brief, hard hug. "Your da will be proud." Without another word, he began to head in the direction of the barn.

Delia turned away from the paddock and began to walk toward the brightly illuminated kitchen. Sounds of talk and laughter floated through an open window. She could see Mary bending over the table with another platter of chicken.

Realizing she was hungry, she increased her speed. As she approached the back door, she gasped as she almost tripped over the figure sitting on the steps.

"Oh!" Strong, male hands caught her by the

waist. She found herself looking up into Morgan's face.

Morgan squinted as he looked down, taking his time to get a better look at Delia's figure in her tight jeans. She was thinner than when he'd lived with her. He didn't like the slightly worried expression that now showed behind her deep blue eyes. She seemed to be stretched taut, her temper ready to flare at any moment.

He had thought it was he who was putting this tension in her demeanor. Tonight he knew for sure.

He had caught enough of her conversation with Tom to know she was talking about him. But he wasn't worried. He had no intention of jeopardizing the picture. They were still right on schedule.

It was the damnedest thing. Normally, he enjoyed the discipline of acting and abhorred prima donnas who held up production with various antics. He had vowed to himself from the very start of his career that he would never be a troublemaker on any set.

Yet here I am, doing exactly that.

What scared him the most was that he was a man who placed great value on being in control. And he had never felt more out of control in his life. Out of control—and vulnerable. To her. And to his own feelings.

"What are you doing here?" Delia launched her attack before Morgan had a chance to say anything.

He reached up and took her chin in his hands, enjoying the soft feel of her skin. He noticed a peculiar look in her eyes. But she held her ground.

"I could ask the same of you. Why don't you watch where you're going?"

She backed away, and he dropped his hand. "Forget it, Morgan. I don't have time to play games with you." She started to brush past him toward the kitchen.

Something inside him snapped. He was tired of being ignored when all his instincts told him she was still attracted to him.

"Delia, wait." When she didn't listen, he grabbed her by the arm and started to drag her away from the kitchen door.

She didn't make a sound, though she twisted and struggled. He held her firmly. Morgan didn't enjoy this. He had simply wanted to talk with her, to try to make her understand what he was feeling. He was frightened, putting his feelings for this woman on the line. But he couldn't stand the tension. He was having a lousy time dealing with his part, with any of his work obligations. It was time they settled their relationship once and for all.

He eased her up against the barn wall. The bright light from inside spilled across her face. She looked up at him with a strange expression. Defiant. Yet vulnerable.

Morgan studied her face, remembering other places, other times: her eyes, wild and excited by passion; her lips, swollen from his kisses; her cheeks, flushed with the aftermath of their love-making.

Without really knowing why he was doing it, he lowered his face to hers.

She twisted away. "Morgan, don't." Her voice was tense. She stood perfectly still. He moved his body slightly, pressing her closer against the barn wall. He could feel every soft curve, could remember the way her body had shaped itself to his.

He turned her face very gently. She had stopped fighting him. Morgan looked into her eyes, trying to find the answer to everything he wanted to ask. He parted his lips and tried to speak.

But he didn't want to. He didn't want to argue or discuss or rationalize. He wanted to make love to her the way he'd dreamed of every night since arriving at the ranch.

As if drawn by an invisible silken cord, he lowered his head and touched his lips to hers.

She resisted at first. He smiled slightly against her mouth as he felt her begin to respond. Maybe this was a good way to settle their differences. Fires as hot as those that had blazed between them couldn't be dampened. He heard himself groan with pleasure as her mouth began to open underneath his. Her sweetness made it hard for him to think clearly. He didn't want to think; he wanted to feel.

He caught her hair in his fingers and gently pulled her closer. Her hands slowly slid up his chest, around his neck as she clasped him against her. The feel of her firm breasts against his chest was a sweet aphrodisiac. He reveled in her closeness, her scent, the feel of her slender body, her trembling warmth. He moved his mouth to her temple, to her cheek, down her neck to the sensitive spot where her pulse raced madly, betraying her. She wasn't indifferent; he knew that. When he heard a small moan escape her lips, the sound excited him further.

"Morgan, no—" Before she could say anything else, he claimed her lips again.

This time he deepened the kiss, slipped his tongue inside her mouth and explored her melting sweetness. She responded in kind. He took pleasure in mastering his passion, holding it in check so she might feel more. He wanted to bring her along slowly, slowly—

He couldn't wait. Morgan felt his hand move, as if with a will of its own. His fingers moved down her shoulder, tenderly caressing, until they cupped her breast. He held her gently, letting her get used to his touch, the intimacy of the caress. When she didn't resist, he began to lightly stroke the tip. It was already hard with desire.

She broke the kiss, turned her face away, put her hand over his. "Morgan, no!"

This time he stopped.

He looked down at her face in the dim light. Flushed and disheveled, Delia seemed beautiful to him. He brought his hand up and traced her lips with a finger.

She flinched and twisted away.

Her action tore at his heart. "Delia, why?"

His voice was soft and low to his ears, reminding him of all their late-night talks in bed. The way she had laughed, then snuggled against his shoulder and fallen asleep, utterly confident in their love.

What had happened to them?

"Delia?"

She didn't answer. He tried to make her face him again, his hand gentle underneath her chin. She wouldn't look at him.

"Delia, we have to talk."

She shrugged her shoulders. After a moment of silence she tried to extricate herself, gingerly. He wouldn't let her go.

"What happened in London?"

This time she turned to look at him. Her bright blue eyes were huge pools of disbelief. She stared at him for just a second, then turned her head away. Her shoulders slumped.

"Morgan, why are you talking about this?"

He sighed. At least she wasn't fighting to be free. "Because I want to know." He cleared his throat, trying to relieve the tightness. "Because I want to know." The hardest part was yet to come, but he forced the words out. "Because I loved you, and—" *Because I still love you. I never realized how much until I saw you on your father's balcony. Because I could give a damn if this picture ever gets made. Because I go to bed at night and can't sleep for thoughts of you in my arms.*

She was staring at him now as if she thought he was crazy. Her body trembled, more violently this time.

"You're cold." Morgan wrapped her more tightly in his arms, close enough to feel her heartbeat. "Let's go inside."

They walked into the warmth and light of the barn. Tom was locking the tack room and heading toward the kitchen. He didn't look up as they entered.

Good man, Tom, Morgan thought. He walked quickly, his arm around Delia, until they were inside a vacant stall. Closing the door behind him, he let her go.

"Why did you leave me in London?" he repeated as he leaned back against the rough wood and watched her.

She looked cornered. "Morgan, you're out of your mind! That was six years ago! Why do we have to discuss the past right now?"

"Because I want to."

"I don't think that—"

"Why did you leave?"

"I'm not going to—"

"Why did you leave me?"

"I don't understand what—"

"Why did you leave me?" The words came out harsher than he'd intended. She stopped talking, just gazed at him mutely. He watched, fascinated, as she began to tremble.

For a moment he thought she was going to run into his arms and surrender. He watched as she came nearer, then suddenly realized the emotion controlling her was more likely to induce violence than surrender. He moved back along the edge of the stall, ducking his head.

"You bastard!" She swung her fist hard enough

to connect with his stomach. He doubled over, grunting with surprise. Morgan tried to reach her, to hold her still, but Delia was a fury to be reckoned with. She darted just out of his reach; then he felt her fists pummeling his back.

"Why the hell did I leave *you*? You have nerve, Morgan! You were gone long before I *ever* left!"

Her relentless anger was palpable; he could feel it. As he moved out of her reach, it took every ounce of his willpower not to strike her. He darted back and looked up to see a dangerous blue fire in her eyes.

"If you were so much 'in love' with me, why didn't you come after me?" She picked up a handful of straw and threw it at him, then flung herself against his chest.

Morgan stumbled and felt his back hit the hardwood box stall. Suddenly it seemed that everything he'd ever really wanted in life was slipping rapidly from his grasp. How could he ever make Delia understand that the intense feelings he had for her had always frightened him? That he hadn't had a lot of experience in loving? That he associated love with weakness and pain, losing and failure? She had been the only brightness in his life, the only person who'd succeeded in reaching beyond the automatic barriers he used to keep people at a distance.

And he was pushing her away.

He had to try. Even if, deep inside, he thought he'd ultimately fail. Because he'd never deserved the gift that was Delia.

He didn't know what to say, what to do, to

make things right and recreate what they'd once had. He wanted to ask her to come back to his room and spend the rest of the evening. The rest of her life.

When he raised his gaze to hers, she was simply staring at him. Her body was perfectly still, but he noticed her hands were trembling before she balled them into tight fists.

Her voice was low, almost inaudible. Ashamed. "I'm sorry, Morgan. I—I was crazy." She looked as if she were about to cry. "I don't know why— It won't happen again."

Before he could reply, she walked quickly out of the stall and down the empty cement corridor.

Chapter Five

Delia could feel her entire body trembling by the time she returned to her room. Locking the door behind her, she dropped down on the bed and buried her face in the pillow.

How could you have responded to his kiss? The thought ran through her mind again and again. She couldn't find any logical answer.

Even after her talk with Tom, even after imagining the way she'd try to be gentle with Morgan, she still hadn't been able to manage things. She was more vulnerable than she'd ever been with him.

Now he knew how she felt. Her body, her deepest feelings—she hadn't been able to lie. Even though she had been exhausted after a day of filming, even though anyone could have walked into the stable at any time during— She groaned and pressed the pillow around her ears, trying to shut out the world.

It was several minutes before she heard soft knocking. Was it Morgan coming after her? She felt her cheeks burn as she remembered the way she'd kissed him, without reserve. *We never had any problems in that area—just all the others.*

"Who's there?"

"Mary."

She got up and unlocked the door, turning quickly away as Mary entered. Delia didn't want her stepmother to suspect her emotions.

"I brought you some dinner. I thought you might be tired and would want to eat in your room." Mary's eyes were serene, unsuspecting. Delia felt the tightness begin to leave her chest. "Thanks. How's Dad?"

"Fine. He's sitting in front of the fire. You might come out later; there's something he wants to talk to you about."

"Give me an hour." She still needed to see the dailies from yesterday's shooting, but they could wait until tomorrow night if James needed her.

"Was it bad today?" Mary's voice was soft, soothing, as she set the tray down on the small bedside table. For a split second, Delia wanted to hug her. She felt as if she were being pulled every which way, with time for no one. Yet Mary took the time to look after her.

She decided not to resist. "Oh, Mary." She enfolded the older woman in her arms and gave her a quick hug. "Thanks so much—for just being here for me."

"Darling, you look as if you're ready to come apart. Is there anything you want to talk about?"

Delia was still for a moment. But then she nodded. "Yes. Not right now. Maybe tonight after Dad goes to bed."

"I'll be up."

After her stepmother left, Delia inspected her food with growing interest. Fried chicken, mashed potatoes, green beans from the garden and a baked apple. Mary had arranged her dinner on the prettiest china. The delicate porcelain had a floral pattern, and the pink-and-white design was restful. Sterling flatware and a linen napkin completed the attractive tray.

She snuggled back in bed and attacked her food. As she ate, she felt she was gaining strength for battles ahead.

A quick shower invigorated her further. Within forty-five minutes she was in the living room with her father.

SHE STILL CARES. There's still something there.

He'd put his feelings on the line, and he'd found the answer he was looking for. But he had to do something to end the endless cycle of tension they were caught up in. Morgan stood looking out the window of his bedroom toward the barn. The stable area was illuminated by several outdoor lights, giving it a strong shape in the middle of darkness.

Mary invited you for tea. Go see Delia before things cool down.

He pressed his palms against his eyes, suddenly tired, not looking forward to another confrontation with Delia.

Just tell her you can't work with her—not with such powerful feelings between you.

So much more than the film was at stake.

JAMES WILDE was lying in a reclining chair, a crocheted afghan around his thin legs. The fire in the huge stone fireplace snapped merrily and gave the dimly lit room a golden glow. King, his German shepherd, lay quietly by the chair.

"Hi, Dad." Delia gave her father a quick kiss on his forehead and sat down on the hassock next to him. "How're you feeling?"

"Not too bad." But his voice sounded rough and tired to Delia's ears. His eyes, deep and alive, captured her attention. James seemed to burn from within. The doctor had told her the cancer was eating him alive. Delia glanced away. She couldn't look at her father at certain times.

"Tom tells me you're having trouble with Morgan."

Delia's head snapped back up quickly, all her senses alert. She gripped the leather of the hassock tightly, kneading the supple material under her tense fingers. "A little bit. But nothing to get worried about."

James laughed softly. "He's a good man, Delia."

She swallowed against the nervous lump in her throat. "I suppose so."

"You need someone strong. Someone who can give you a real run for your money."

Oh, he did. "Oh, come on, Daddy!" She could tell the familiar endearment pleased him. He reached for her hand and patted it clumsily.

"I don't want to think about leaving you alone."

The tears were just behind her eyes now.

"Nonsense. I'll have Mary." *I can't bear to talk about this.*

James made a sound, half growl, half laugh. "That's not what I mean, and you know it. It's time you found yourself a man and settled down." When she didn't answer, he continued gently, "I haven't much time, so I've got to say what needs to be said now."

"I'm not mad at you."

"Take a good look at Morgan, Cordelia. He's attracted to you. I could see it if my eyes were closed."

I know. But for all the wrong reasons. "Attracted or not, I wish he'd listen when I ask him to do things on the set."

"He'll respect you in time." James closed his eyes. "He's just having difficulty because you're a beautiful woman."

Delia didn't answer. For a time they sat in front of the fire, bathed in warmth and silence, the only sound the rattle and hiss of the flames.

"You remind me of your mother."

Delia almost jumped off her seat at the sound of his voice. Seeing her father's tired and concerned face, she smiled. "Sorry, Dad. I'm just worn out."

"I called her the other night."

"You did?" She tried to keep the amazement out of her voice. Delia couldn't remember the last time her parents had spoken. While attending private school in Paris, she had read various accounts of the divorce. The articles had been unanimous in one respect—James and Danielle's parting had been very bitter.

He nodded, his large head barely moving. "I had to tell her, Delia. I couldn't let her read about it in the papers."

"What did she say?" The question slipped out before she thought he might not want her to know. Some things were too private.

But her curiosity didn't seem to bother James. "She started to cry. Then she began talking in French, very fast—you remember?" He smiled and closed his eyes again, as if retreating to an inner world of memories and dreams. "I calmed her down—" Delia smiled. James had always calmed Danielle down. Volatile and completely French, her mother had derived a measure of serenity from James. "And we talked."

"What did you talk about?" Delia was fascinated. She had never thought of her parents this way.

"We talked about you."

"Oh."

He reached for her hand this time, as if to prevent her from pulling away. "She told me about Morgan. Don't look so astonished. I'd suspected for a while. The way he looked at you at my party, the way you act like a cat with her back up whenever he comes into a room— Delia, darling, whatever is the matter with you?"

"I'm so sorry, Daddy. It's just—" With an angry gesture she wiped away the tears sliding down her cheeks. "Just that I never turned out the way you wanted me to. I should have given you grandchildren. I should have—"

"You were always *exactly* what I wanted. Don't you ever forget that." He sighed, and the breath seemed to go through his entire body. "If I leave you with nothing else, remember you've given me a great amount of joy."

She could barely see the room through the blur of tears. Delia admitted defeat and began to cry.

She felt James's warm, rough hands on her shoulders, and then she was cradled in his arms. The fire had burned down to embers, and Delia was thankful for any added measure of darkness to hide her turbulent emotions.

She felt him push a handkerchief into her fingers, and she accepted it gratefully. Delia blew her nose and wiped her face, then stuffed the cloth into her back pocket.

"I'm sorry—"

"Don't be. I want to tell you something." He coughed, then grimaced. "I have to tell you something." He reached down absently and began to scratch behind King's ears. "There are times when I feel I haven't been a very good father to you—"

"Stop it!"

He held up a hand. "Calm down. There are times—" he hesitated for a fraction of a second "—when I wonder if I was there for you when you needed me."

She knew he was referring to the time she'd

fled London and come to live at the ranch. James had been working and hadn't come home until almost a month later. Mary had put the pieces of her emotions together, very slowly.

"You were there as much as you could be. I never thought of you as an absent father."

"But I was. I was so hell-bent on my damn career. I thought the sun rose and set depending on what part I was given to play. And now I'm wondering if the part of father and husband was my poorest performance."

"No." She tried to smile reassuringly, but her mouth felt shaky. "I can't believe you're talking like this."

He leaned back into his chair. "Delia, I always thought that someday I would sum up my life. I just didn't think it would be this soon. When I think about dying, there's so much I realize I didn't do!"

"But look at what you did!"

James stared at Delia squarely, and she thought she saw a glimmer of his former self. The strength, the power, of the man was present for just an instant before it vanished. "But the things I didn't do were important. And I want you to know this while you still have time."

"Daddy, what are you talking about?"

"Do I have to spell it out for you, Delia? Are you daft? The man's in love with you! You both made a mistake once. Danielle didn't tell me everything. I don't know why you left him. But it's harder for a man to admit that he's wrong."

She sat, silent, unable to speak:

"He's an actor, yes, but an actor like me!"
James's eyes blazed for a second; then the inner
fire was extinguished. "Sometimes we act to forget who we are, to be able to lose ourselves in
someone else's emotions for a moment of peace.
Compared to feeling our own, it's easy."

"He doesn't love me. He only wants to—"
She stopped, horrified.

James started to laugh. "Oh, I can see that,
too. But it's more than sexual. The two of you
are perfectly suited. Neither of you has lived an
ordinary life. You'd be a constant source of
amusement, of love, of excitement."

"What about you and Mother?" Her attack
was out of her mouth with lightning speed. An
instant later she regretted it.

"That's a fair question. Your mother and I
married—"

"Because of me."

His eyes widened a fraction. "Who told you
that?"

"Mother. So now we're even."

James studied her face thoughtfully. "Danielle was pregnant, yes. But you came at a good
time. You made us come to a decision about
where we were going, what we had to do with
our lives."

"But you left her!"

"We left each other." His eyes were dark with
remembered pain.

Delia had to ask. It was something she had
wondered about all her life. "Do you ever
wonder— Do you sometimes think it might

have worked? You and Mother, I mean?'' She sniffed, then reached for her handkerchief. She could feel her nose starting to stuff up.

"No." For an instant Delia thought she detected a spasm of pain flicker across the strong leonine features. "I wasn't very good for your mother."

"Oh." Delia paused for a second, then rushed on. "Sometimes I think I'm not very good for Morgan."

"You're very good for him. He needs a woman who doesn't run into a corner the second he bursts into a temper."

Remembering their fight in the stall, Delia started to laugh. "I don't know. Maybe he's no good for me." She looked at her father, wondering if he would agree.

"He's *perfect* for you." James seemed content now that he'd said what he wanted to say.

"I knew you'd be prejudiced—you actors stick together."

James cleared his throat and began to speak in a soft, melodious voice. "'As an imperfect actor on the stage, who with his fear is put besides his part.'"

The sounds of the Shakesperean sonnet filled the room, his resonant actor's voice making the words come alive with emotion and meaning.

"'So I, for fear of trust, forget to say, the perfect ceremony of love's rite.'"

Delia closed her eyes, letting the words wash over her. Trust James to speak to her through poetry.

"'O, learn to read what silent love hath writ:
To hear with eyes belongs to love's fine wit.'"

The last syllable of the sonnet faded as Delia
looked at her father. If a person could look love
in the face, this would be it. So much of James
had gone into that simple little recital: his love of
the language, his beautiful speaking voice, his
fondness for Shakespeare and his characters. But
most important, his ability to communicate the
love and the subtle message to Delia. James
could have come right out and said it; he pre-
ferred, as always, the actor's mask.

She reached over and took his hand, squeezed
it slowly. Words were useless. What he had
given her was so precious.

The gentle slapping of house slippers against
the hardwood floors jolted Delia out of her
thoughts. Mary came into the room, bearing a
tray of freshly baked brownies.

James broke the spell. "Mary, my dear. We
were just talking by the fire." He sat up and attempted to arrange the afghan.

Delia was at his side instantly, tucking the
wool material around his thinning legs.

"How lovely of you to bring tea." James's
voice was warm and inviting, and it was then that
Delia realized the three of them weren't alone.
James continued to speak.

"Morgan, how nice of you to stop by."

She didn't want to look at him. Not after what
had happened in the stable.

James continued talking, seemingly unaware
of the tension in the room. "I was going to call

you and ask if you'd mind running lines with me tonight.''

She couldn't avoid him any longer without being inexcusably rude. The words faded; sounds became meaningless as Delia glanced up and saw Morgan's dark face. His eyes surprised her. Warm, filled with an almost tender light. It was a look she'd never seen before.

She fought the urge to run, to clamp down her emotions before they could carry her away on a tide of pure feeling.

Sitting down on the hassock at her father's feet, Delia leaned over the coffee table and picked up the plump red earthenware pot Morgan had set down. She started to pour. ''Mary, sit down. You look exhausted.'' Amazingly, her hand was steady. ''Morgan, would you put another log on the fire?''

She watched him covertly as he replenished the flames. The room blazed to golden life once again.

When he moved to sit beside her on the hassock, she didn't even flinch; she simply handed him a cup of tea. The gesture made her think of countless times they had performed this intimate ritual in London. Another quick look at his face let her know Morgan remembered, too.

''To hear with eyes...'' She could only try.

An hour later, Delia leaned back into the couch, her stomach comfortably full of tea and chocolate brownies. The fire had a somnolent effect, and she felt her eyelids growing heavy. James's and Morgan's voices were somewhere in the background as they ran their lines back and forth. The two men played with the language, delivering the dialogue in different ways, stopping to talk about background, motivation, point of view. Even just hearing the lines, Delia knew that a special, indefinable chemistry existed between the actors.

My instincts were right. At least about this. She tilted her head back against the soft cushions. Why was the room so warm? The events of the past twenty-four hours were catching up with a vengeance. She closed her eyes and let the voices fade into a soft buzzing around her head.

"WAKE UP, SLEEPYHEAD." Delia heard a soft voice that sounded as if it were coming from far away. She moved and tried to hunch down inside herself. But the hands and voice were insistent.

"What?" She opened her eyes to find Morgan's face very close to her own. His dark eyes were scrutinizing her with tender amusement.

She sat up, pushing her hair off her face with a heavy arm. "Where's Dad?" Her voice sounded breathy to her ears.

"He went to bed. We finished running lines about an hour ago, but I didn't have the heart to wake you."

"Oh." The thought of Morgan watching her while she slept was oddly disquieting. Delia stood up, as much to relieve the stiffness of her limbs as to put some space between them. She stretched lazily, then tucked her shirt back into her jeans. "I'd better be heading to bed myself. We've got a long day of shooting ahead."

Morgan patted the cushions beside him. "Give me a few minutes, Delia. We have to talk... please."

It was the last thing she wanted to do, but how could she refuse him when he asked so politely? She eased herself back down on the couch, watching him all the while.

"I'm not going to bite." He sounded tired.

"Okay." She folded her arms in front of her, as if the simple gesture could offer a measure of protection.

Morgan paused for an instant. She thought she detected a glimmer of uncertainty in his eyes, then decided against it. What did Morgan have to be uncertain of? It seemed as if he always held the upper hand in any of their encounters. She tightened her arms around her body.

The fire had burned low, the glowing embers sending out the only light in the room. Flickering shadows danced across Morgan's face, across the hard jaw, the sculpted bones. She wanted to reach out and touch that face as she had so many times in her dreams. But she kept her arms firmly crossed.

"Delia, I'm having a very hard time working with you on this film."

She felt herself begin to bristle but bit her lips against the flow of words threatening to spill out of her mouth. *That makes two of us, Morgan.* She remained silent, wishing her heart wouldn't beat quite so fast. He wasn't even touching her. Though not much space separated them on the couch, he didn't need to have a hand on her. She could feel his warmth and sensuality from a distance, as if he were a magnetic field reaching toward her, trying to draw her against him.

Delia straightened up further against the soft cushions. She twisted the weight of her hair away from her face. "It hasn't been easy for me either, Morgan. But this picture is very important to me." Could she tell him why?

"I know you may not believe this, but I never stopped loving you." His dark eyes were intense, full of emotion.

She didn't know what to say. Delia looked down, afraid that he might see his answer in her eyes. When had she started to care again? Had she ever really stopped? How long would it take for her to admit to herself she still loved him?

The thought shocked her into looking up again. He was watching her, and there was a new softness about his face that shook her far more than his fierceness. If Morgan held power over her when he was intense and demanding, he was devastating in his vulnerability.

"I don't believe you stopped loving me, either." Morgan simply stated it as a fact. Delia couldn't deny the truth. He was meeting her more than halfway.

"Yes." She nodded her head slightly, keeping her eyes on his face. A soft warmth began blooming deep within her body.

He shifted his weight, stretching his legs in

front of him. Morgan stared into the dying fire for several minutes. Delia shivered slightly, and he turned toward her.

"Cold?"

She nodded. She wasn't really, but she needed time to think. Her emotions always got her into trouble where Morgan was concerned. Delia watched as Morgan put another small log on the fire. The flames began to bloom, soft, yellow-white tongues that licked around the aromatic wood.

Delia couldn't take her eyes off the easy, sensual way he moved. As he walked back toward the couch, she leaned back against the cushions. Their softness didn't offer much support.

"Come here." He patted the space next to him.

She remained where she was, watching him warily. Though Morgan had made a verbal declaration of his feelings, she still didn't trust him. If she was really truthful, she didn't trust herself. Why did she have to go all soft when it came to this man? She decided to change the subject.

"Your lines sounded good. The scene shouldn't take too long to shoot."

He frowned. She felt rather than saw him lean toward her. His hand caught hers, and he pulled gently until she came to rest in his arms. She lay very still, almost afraid of making any movement. Delia felt his hand touch her gently; then he began to stroke her hair.

The house was so quiet, the only sound the faint cry of the wind outside, the hissing of the fire within. She began to relax against him, to float on a cloud of familiar, pure sensuality. She didn't resist as his fingers tightened in her hair, tilting her head back as his lips moved over hers.

In that instant she lost all rational thought. Her hand left his to slide up the firm, muscular wall of his chest, to the back of his neck and into the soft hair at his shirt collar. There had never been a man she had enjoyed touching more than Morgan. Her other hand soon clasped the first as she steadied herself against him.

It was a soft kiss, a slow kiss. He was giving her plenty of time to respond. She moved closer and parted her lips to deepen the intimacy between them.

She felt him ease her down on the couch, then slide one leg over both of hers. His lips left hers; his head came up slowly. She opened her eyes to see what was the matter and saw him looking at her with an odd expression on his face.

She reacted to the change instantly. Her body stiffened, and she pulled slightly away. What did he really want from her?

"Delia." His voice was tight. "I don't think I can work with you on a professional level with this between us."

The silence stretched after his whispered, agonized confession. She stared up into his face, not believing what she had just heard.

Slowly, feeling as if she might break apart at any moment, she slid from beneath his leg, got up off the couch and walked over to James's chair by the fire. Sitting down, she studied her hands for a moment, then looked up.

"What is it exactly that you want from me?" Her voice sounded dull to her ears. She knew now that she'd been dreading this moment, this choice, from the moment she'd seen him again. He had wanted her off the picture from the beginning. His work always came first. Why couldn't he trust her? What he was asking her to do was impossible, and she couldn't explain. Morgan could never understand how she felt about this film.

He started to move toward her, but she glared at him, and he remained where he was. "Delia, you don't understand—"

"I'm glad we can agree on that at least." Her words were clipped, frosty. Feeling hurt beyond measure, she kept her voice low and controlled. "Now tell me, why is it you can't work with me?" She was amazed at how steady her voice sounded when she felt as if her heart were breaking.

He laughed, shakily. "I've never been in love with my director before."

She shook her head. "I'm not buying that, Morgan."

For an instant she thought she saw pain cross his features. But then his face settled into the hard mask she knew only too well, concealing whatever emotions might be beneath the surface.

"Why does directing this film mean so much to you?" he asked harshly. "And why are you so unconcerned about how I feel?"

"I'm not unconcerned. It's just impossible for me to get a replacement."

"I could ask Joseph Bates to fly up and finish filming." He was sitting forward, his hands clasped tightly in front of him.

You bastard. You had my replacement all picked and ready. Delia stiffened with rage at the mention of their mutual friend. She knew Joe all too well. If he had his way the film would be nothing but a shoot-'em-up Western. She couldn't do that to James. Or herself. The film she wanted to create dealt with human emotions and relationships on a large, dramatic scale—not who was the fastest gun in the West. She wanted to give James one last great character before he died.

"No." She stood up. "I'm sorry. You'll have to understand, Morgan, that I take my work as seriously as you do."

His eyes glittered angrily in the firelight. His next words seemed to be torn out from an anger deep within rather than spoken from the heart. Yet they were no less final. "Then you may have to find yourself another actor."

"Fine." Delia's voice shook as she gathered her pride to shield herself from the pain that would make itself felt after the shock of their angry words wore off. Trembling inside, she walked quickly out of the room. She heard Morgan leave, then went back into the living room. Checking the fire, then making sure the house was secure for the night, she made her way quietly down the dark hall.

But once in bed, she couldn't sleep. Morgan's

face, his voice, haunted her through the night.
He said he loved her. But he couldn't work with
her.

There was no answer.

*You're right, Morgan. I am doing this film partly
for myself. I have to show James how much I love
him. I have to believe that I was good enough to be
his daughter.*

Delia tossed restlessly in bed, punching her
pillow and burying her face in it, trying to shut
off her feelings. Perhaps she could handpick
another director, one whose vision of the picture
was closer to her own.

But I can't.

At intervals, she would glance at the luminous
dial on her alarm clock. Before long, morning
began to wash her bedroom with muted color.
And Delia was still no closer to a solution.

It was almost six before she gave in and realized sleep was impossible. Pulling on jeans and a
T-shirt, then a heavy gray sweatshirt with a
hood, she let herself out of the house and
walked toward the corral.

Tom was already up. She could smell the distinct scent of strong coffee coming from his office.

"Couldn't sleep?" His pale blue eyes were
gentle as he handed her a cup.

She nodded her head. "I'm going to ride
down by the creek."

"It's a good morning for it." Tom took a long
swallow of his coffee and set the cup down.
"Which beast did you have in mind?"

"Falstaff."

"Good. He needs the work." Tom gestured toward his desk. "Prop your feet up and have another cup. Mary left me some of her brownies if you're hungry. I'll saddle him up and bring him around."

"Thank you, Tom."

Surprisingly, she was hungry. The coffee and chocolate revived her, and when she heard the firm clip-clop of hooves against cement, she joined Tom in the corridor.

"Would you tell Mary I'll be back in time for breakfast?" She looped the reins around the saddle horn and vaulted up onto Falstaff's broad back.

"I'll make sure of it." Tom backed away and gave her a wave of his hand. "Whatever's making you frown, I hope it leaves you by the time you get back."

She smiled and gave him a quick salute.

The morning air was chilly and damp. Delia eased the massive quarter horse into a trot, then a gentle canter and into the back field. Falstaff moved like a gigantic rocking horse, and the gentle rolling motion helped to assuage her feelings of anger and helplessness. She forgot everything as she moved into the stallion's rhythm.

When she reached the creek, she dismounted and dropped the reins, letting Falstaff graze on some sweet clover. Walking over to the creek bed, she squatted down on her heels and studied the surface of the water.

The bright morning sunlight danced over the

restless water, turning the surface into a brilliantly faceted, liquid jewel. She felt the ground behind her for a dry spot, then sat down.

What to do. She stared at the mountain range in the distance, trying to form an answer in her mind. Delia gathered a certain amount of serenity from the majestic range, from the ribbon of aspen trees at their base to the evergreens higher up. But it was the sheer, craggy granite faces that she studied. She could get lost looking at the mountains when her brain raced feverishly, and she did that now, letting the sculptured, rough edges soothe her soul and calm the desperate worry within her heart.

But there wasn't any question in her mind. Morgan or no Morgan, the picture had to be completed. *And there isn't anyone who can do as good a job as I can.* It wasn't a conceited thought, just a simple realization of the truth. This film was a labor of love, straight from the heart. How could anyone else understand?

She could tell Morgan about Dad. He would understand her need to direct the picture then. But did she have that right? James was such a private man. And he had been so excited last night by the energy he and Morgan had brought to the line reading. Would knowing about James's condition change Morgan's attitude toward the older actor, even slightly? It was something she didn't have the right to risk.

Delia picked up a small, smooth stone and plunked it into the water. She leaned back on her elbows and looked back at the horizon. In the distance, the granite-faced mountains loomed on the horizon. Gigantic. Invincible. It was strange to think they would be here long after James died. After all of them were gone.

Falstaff whickered. She turned her head to check him. The animal was still contentedly grazing. Delia lay down and closed her eyes against the pale sunshine.

The warmth, the sound of water rushing over stone, the gentle morning breeze, all combined to relax and refresh her spirit. She lay still for a short time, then got back up and headed for her mount.

Up on Falstaff's broad back, Delia clicked her tongue gently until he broke into a trot. She knew he would find his way back to the barn without direction from her.

Delia's thoughts drifted toward a solution, but none was in sight. Morgan might hate her, but she couldn't give over the picture to anyone. She had to do this for James. And herself. There would be time for her relationship with Morgan later, and he would realize why she had to do the picture on such a tight schedule.

Was it fate trying to warn her? She and Morgan had never been together at the right time; their relationship had never been easy. Would there ever be a time when they wouldn't be in conflict, could simply be together? All they seemed to do was hurt each other.

He might be leaving today, anyway. Then you

won't have to worry anymore. But did she want that? How would she explain Morgan's absence to James?

She could see the barn on the horizon. Hades was out in the corral, galloping around the enclosure. She squinted her eyes and made out Tom and Morgan leaning against the rail.

She squeezed her knees gently against Falstaff's sides, and he broke into a canter toward home.

Get it over with.

Chapter Six

The corral seemed to rush up to meet her. Dismounting, Delia handed the reins to Tom. Their nonverbal communication had always been excellent, and today was no exception. She was sure he sensed she needed to be alone to talk with Morgan. As man and quarter horse headed in the direction of the barn, she faced Morgan.

His expression was that bland, smooth mask she hated. Delia had to admit there had been times when she'd deliberately goaded him, wanting to see that coolness fade, to be replaced by a quick flash of passion. Anything but this controlled stranger.

"Did you decide?" he asked.

She watched him carefully for any signs that he might wish to take back his ultimatum. "There's a flight back to Los Angeles at ten this morning," she replied. "If you can be packed by eight, one of the men can run you to the airport."

There might have been a slight stiffening of his body, but his face didn't change at all. Hating his control, she watched as he turned toward the rail and rested his arms along the top. His eyes remained on Hades as he replied.

"So you're staying on," he continued in the same flat tone.

"Yes." Her voice was calm, but part of her was dying inside. She wanted him to stay so desperately. But was it for James's sake—or her own?

"Why are you doing this, Delia?"

She almost lost all control at that moment. The hint of pain that had broken through his mask tore at her heart. Delia wanted to tell him. When she'd lived with Morgan, she had always shared her problems with him. They had talked so many nights away, long after they should have been asleep. It had been like slipping into a second skin, warm and reassuring. And she needed someone to share the painful secret of James's dying.

But she didn't. Instead, trying to communicate some of her hurt and fear, she touched him lightly on the arm. "I have to. If I don't do this film, Morgan, I'll never be able to live with myself. Please try to understand."

Before he could reply, she heard the screen door off the kitchen slam. Turning in the direction of the house, Delia caught her breath as she saw James walking slowly toward them. She couldn't bear to see her father hurt. He had been delighted when Morgan had agreed to do the film. Now he would have to be told he was leaving.

She didn't say anything as James came up to the rail and leaned companionably next to them. The tightness in her throat prevented any words.

Easing the air past her constricted throat, she decided to get it over with. Delia glanced up at her father. "Morgan has something to tell you, Dad."

James seemed pleased as he turned toward the younger man. "I could certainly use some good news."

For once, Delia noted with satisfaction, *he's shaken*. She'd seen Morgan's eyes widen just a fraction, seen his lips tighten when she'd spoken. The silence seemed to stretch forever. Delia waited for him to speak, her heart in her mouth as she waited for the man she loved to hurt the father she loved.

The silence seemed to stretch forever, until Morgan finally spoke. "Delia said we could begin shooting our first scene today."

For an endless moment she thought she hadn't heard him correctly. Then, when his words finally sank in, she put her hand on his arm and gave it the gentlest squeeze.

Thank you, Morgan. For giving us another chance.

SHE CALLED YOUR BLUFF, so make the most of it.

Morgan had never thought she'd stand up to him. But the Delia directing this film was a different woman from the girl he'd known six years ago.

He was standing by the corral fence, watching

Hades restlessly move around the small enclosure.

I know just how you feel, he thought.

His time at the ranch was turning out to be much more pleasant than he'd thought. Mary and James seemed to accept him. He'd had quite a few conversations with Tom, had watched him work with the Arabian stallion a few mornings. He admired the man and his talent.

He held his hand out over the rail, and Hades approached cautiously. Mary had given him an apple, and he'd eaten most of it. But he wanted to see if Hades would approach.

When he felt velvety lips tickle the palm of his hand, he murmured softly, "You're braver than I am, boy."

Watching the stallion move to the center of the corral, he dug his hands into his jeans pockets.

Let go of the fear. Stop letting it run you.

So much easier said than done.

The least he could do was grow up and start behaving on the set. Delia had made it very clear she wasn't going to back down. And he admired her for it.

"THAT'S A WRAP!" Delia called out, delighted with the results. Walking quickly in front of the camera, she looped her arm through her father's and smiled up at him. "You're really cooking."

James was truly in his element. "It had a lot to do with this man." He gestured over to Morgan, standing only four feet away.

"Thank you, Morgan. That last take was excellent, and I'm sure we're going to use it." Facing everyone, hands resting gently on her hips, she shouted, "That's it for today! I'll see you all at eight tomorrow morning!"

She turned away from Morgan, concentrating on her father. James looked good today. His deep blue eyes, so like her own, were sparkling, and there was a ruddy glow high on his cheeks. But Delia also knew he had an almost superhuman ability to concentrate on a given scene. She didn't know how much longer his strength would last.

She was grateful when she saw Tom walk quickly to James's side and question her with his eyes. She nodded, the gesture almost imperceptible. Without speaking, Tom clapped James on the shoulder, and the two older men began to walk slowly back toward the pickup truck Tom had driven out to location.

Delia was so caught up in watching them leave that she jumped when she felt a pair of strong, warm hands settle on her shoulders.

"I have to admit, you're really pulling it out of him. That was the best I've ever seen James."

She wished she could have told him it had little or nothing to do with her direction. A dying man couldn't afford to play it safe, to wait passively before he made his move. James knew this was the performance he would be remembered for.

"Thank you. You're pretty hot stuff yourself."

He laughed then, throwing back his head and looking more boyish than he had in a long time. The tight lines of tension at his mouth temporarily eased, and when he looked back down at her, there was a relaxed sparkle in his dark eyes.

"You've got guts, Delia. You may just make it, after all."

She decided to play along, liking this new side of him. Ever since Morgan had decided to stay, he'd been like a new man. He had never done anything halfway, and now he threw himself into his work with his usual intensity, concentration and attention to detail. He was much closer to the man she'd known so long ago. Had it really been only six years ago? It seemed that their relationship was blooming all over again, and it certainly felt the same.

Sticking her hands into her back pockets, she grinned up at him. "We'd better hurry if we're going to catch dinner."

He surprised her then, taking one of her arms and gently pulling her hand out of her pocket, then linking his fingers through hers. Squeezing her hand, he said, "I've got an even better idea."

"What?" She couldn't help her heartbeat speeding up just a fraction or the way her breath caught in her throat.

"I thought we might go out to dinner tonight."

She couldn't resist. "Won't Belinda be lonely?"

He mock scowled. "She won't even notice I'm gone, believe me."

"Do I get a chance to clean up, or do you want me smelling like a horse?"

His dark eyes were suddenly serious. "I'll take you any way I can get you."

She looked away. "Why don't we head back so we can both change."

He laughed, deep in his throat, then reached a gentle finger underneath her chin, tilting her face up to his. "Why don't you join me in the shower?" His voice was a liquid caress, warm and inviting. Full of promise.

Delia knew the only way she'd be able to deal with him was to keep things on a humorous level. "But then we'd never make it to dinner." She reached up for his hand underneath her chin and gave it a teasing push. "Meet me in the living room in an hour, okay?"

It was the fastest hour she'd ever lived through. Between racing back to the house, jumping into a hot shower, washing and blow-drying her hair and trying on six different outfits, she was barely ready on time. But Delia finally settled on a cranberry hand-knit sweater and a mid-calf length black skirt and boots. Tired of her constant wardrobe of jeans and sweats, she wanted to dress up and forget all her worries. And she wanted Morgan to appreciate her as a woman and forget she was his director.

The expression in his eyes was reward enough. He devoured her. As he helped her into her jacket, his fingertips gently brushed the back of her neck, and Delia felt warm and liquid as sudden desire shot through her body.

"Don't wait up," she called to Mary. Miraculously, her voice didn't tremble.

They drove into Jackson, past the numerous hotels, bars and restaurants. It was a city designed for tourists, with an older section resembling a frontier town and stores containing western gear, souvenirs and backpacking equipment. It was always crowded in the summer, when so many tourists came to see Yellowstone. Delia always marveled at the contrast between the isolation of the ranch and the quicker, more festive feeling of the town.

Morgan asked her to recommend a restaurant, and she chose a steak house where the food was good, solid and unpretentious. After a simple meal of steak and salad, they faced each other over coffee.

"You've changed," he said softly.

"Good or bad?" She tried not to let him see how important his opinion was to her.

"Both." He took a sip of his coffee, his eyes never leaving her face.

"Tell me."

"You're more confident. You're much more in control than you used to be. I like that."

Strange that it should seem that way to him when this entire time she'd felt she was totally out of control.

"Go on."

"But—" He seemed to be picking his words very carefully.

"Morgan," she said lightly, placing her hand over his. "You won't hurt me."

He took a deep breath. "You seem harder. As if nothing can get to you. And the picture—it's almost an obsession."

"It is," she admitted. "I'll be relieved when it's over." And suddenly she realized she meant more than the film itself. She would be relieved when James wouldn't be facing pain every day. When she and Mary would be able to look at each other and realize the waiting was over.

"Why did you recommend me for the part?" he asked suddenly.

Delia was about to reply with the fact that it had been for James. But she couldn't. She wanted to be honest with Morgan, even if it would hurt later.

"I wanted to see you again."

He paused for a second, and when he spoke, his voice was quiet and intense.

"Did you miss me as much as I missed you?"

She nodded her head. "I missed you terribly."

"I thought about you—all the time. When I teased you about the three films— I used to watch the papers carefully to make sure I didn't miss a single one of the films you directed. I felt as if they were a tiny link to you. That you were still real to me as long as I knew you were out there somewhere, working."

She couldn't believe Morgan was opening up to her like this. It was a conversation that demanded nothing but honesty. "I saw all of your films, too. It was the same for me. I kept telling myself you looked so good, you were doing so well. And that made me happy."

"I wasn't doing that well," he admitted in a low voice. "I always kept hoping you'd come back."

"You didn't want me then, Morgan. I was only in the way."

"That's not true." He placed his hand over hers, and she enjoyed the warmth, the slight pressure. "I always wanted you."

"You were never home," she reminded him gently.

"There's a time for building a career, and there's a time for enjoying it," he said softly. "We were both building then, but you hadn't decided on a direction. I couldn't help it if things started to catch fire."

"Why couldn't you have told me that then?" she asked, her throat unbearably tight. They had talked about everything but what had mattered most.

"I didn't even know it." He squeezed her hand. "Six years is a long time, Delia. Especially when you're part of a life that lets you experience everything. There were so many things I regret about that time with you." As she started to pull her hand away, his grip tightened. "Not about you. About the way I handled things. About the way I let pride get in the way so much of the time. I was so caught up in forging the direction of my own life that I missed the way yours was going." He smiled sadly. "And the direction you took was straight out of my life."

"Why didn't you ever even call me?" she asked.

His mouth tightened. "This may still be very hard for you to understand, but at the time I resented who you were terribly. James Wilde's daughter. You had everything in the world. How could I possibly have provided for you? It was all right when we were playing house in London. But the one thing I wanted to do more than anything was to ask you to marry me."

She couldn't say anything; she was stunned by his admission. Not knowing what else to do and wanting to hold the moment, she laced her fingers through his and held on tightly as he continued.

"And what could I have offered you? A little flat in London that barely had hot water half the time? A chance to spend the rest of your life wearing bargain-basement clothing?" Lingering bitterness colored his words. "I wouldn't have taken any of his money if I'd married you, Delia. I wanted to provide for you. I needed to provide for you."

He talked rapidly, quietly, as if he had missed his chance before and it had stayed all bottled up inside for the past six years. If there was any chance for their future, it had to be said now.

"You had a family, and it was obvious even to me that you were an adored child. I had no family to offer you, not even a bad one. I thought I pulled you down. Debased you. And I couldn't do that, Delia. Not the way I felt about you."

"Why couldn't you tell me any of this before?"

"I didn't even know most of it consciously. All I knew was that I thought you deserved better, so I did everything in my power to push you out of my life. And at the same time I kept trying to prove myself to you, that I was good enough for you. It was all that ever mattered to me."

"I know that feeling," she said. "I feel that way about my father all the time. It's always been like a series of tests. And deep inside I feel like I don't always measure up."

He squeezed their still-linked hands in sympathy and understanding. As the conversation lagged, Delia started to feel an electric tension building slowly from their linked fingers. She withdrew hers, not sure if she was ready to deal with the physical side of their new, tentative relationship.

"I think we'd better get back," she said softly. "There's a lot of work we have to get done tomorrow."

Without a word, he signaled their waiter and paid the bill. Once inside Mary's station wagon, Morgan turned on the heat and began to drive slowly back to the ranch.

It was as if he were reluctant to see their evening come to an end. Delia was surprised he'd opened up so much in the course of one evening. Was this the same man who had such a deliberately bland expression in the face of intense emotion? It didn't seem possible.

They parked the car outside the garage, then walked slowly toward the house. The stars were bright overhead, like sparks of crystal on a silken bed. A gentle breeze blew the scent of crisp mountain air around them. Delia pulled her jacket tighter.

"You don't have to walk me to the house. I'm okay now."

Morgan tightened his grip on her arm. "I'll see you to your door."

When they reached the kitchen door, Delia stepped up onto the cement step so that she was almost level with Morgan's eyes. "I had a wonderful time, Morgan. It meant so much to me that—that we could talk like that."

He didn't reply, but the pressure of his hand on her arm increased slightly.

"Good night," she whispered. Then, obeying a total impulse, she leaned forward and kissed him gently on his cheek.

She heard his quickly indrawn breath; then his fingers tightened on her elbow. He moved slowly as his arms encircled her; then he just held her. She could feel his heart pounding, the warmth of his breath on her neck. Delia didn't move. She wanted to stay with him forever.

"Come back with me." He spoke so softly she almost didn't hear him.

"Morgan—"

"Not to make love. Just to sleep with me. I want to hold you next to me all night."

She hesitated for a second, but Delia knew it was what she wanted, too. She didn't want the special feeling between them to end. Not yet. But she knew she was playing with fire.

"I promise," he breathed softly. "Just to hold you. Nothing else."

She'd always been able to trust his word. Perhaps things could work if they took each step slowly. She thought of Tom and Hades, the painstaking steps in the frightened Arabian's training.

And we're both frightened. Unsure. But Morgan's taken the first step, and I want to meet him halfway. More than halfway.

She slid her arms up his chest until they encircled his neck, then lay her cheek against his shoulder. "Yes."

He picked her up easily and carried her around the side of the house, toward the guest house. Mary had moved Belinda to one of the guest bedrooms in the main house, so Morgan had the little house all to himself.

He maneuvered the door open gently, then carried her over the threshold as carefully as if she were a china figurine. Shutting the door firmly behind him, he walked quickly into the darkened bedroom.

Delia tensed for just an instant as he lay her down on the bed. The mattress gave gently, springs squeaking. Then he sat down next to her and began to take off his shirt. She moved to help him, but he took her hand and held it tightly.

"No. I'm not that much of a saint," he whispered.

Understanding, she stood up and began to unzip her skirt. She slid the zipper down carefully, and she stepped out of it, then drew her sweater over her head and stepped out of her boots. Clad only in her silk slip, bra, bikini and stockings, she turned her back on Morgan and reached behind her for the fastening of her bra. As the straps slid down over her upper arms, she looked over her shoulder and saw him lying on the bed, bare chested, watching her.

"You're just as beautiful as I remembered," he said softly.

She turned away, and her bra joined her skirt and sweater on the chair.

She removed her stockings, then her slip, then finally her tiny lace bikini. Feeling strangely shy—hadn't she slept in the same bed with Morgan hundreds of times—she sat down on the edge of the bed. A heartbeat later, she felt his hand on her waist, his fingers warm.

"Climb in. You must be freezing."

She moved underneath the covers, grateful to be able to cover her nakedness. The sheets were warm from when Morgan had been lying on top of the bed. Delia closed her eyes as she heard the sound of a zipper, then soft thuds as Morgan's clothes hit the floor.

She felt the bed give slightly as he lay down, then a brief rush of air as the covers were opened. And then he was beside her, his body warm and hard, comforting in the darkness.

"Come here," he whispered.

She turned toward him. He was holding out an arm, and she went to him, burying her face against his chest, loving the feel of his rough hair on her cheek. She sighed softly, the sound loud in the quiet room.

"This is what I missed the most." Morgan's breath tickled her ear.

"Me, too."

He moved his hand slowly down her back until he cupped her buttocks gently. It was as if he were rediscovering her body all over again. Delia was glad they had time. Their kiss had been rushed, desperate. Now, though they weren't going to make love, they had time to be truly intimate.

She sighed as he pulled her closer against him, then kissed her forehead and smoothed her hair away.

"Thank you for coming back with me."

She kissed the tender skin just underneath his ear. "My pleasure." When his arm tightened around her, she whispered, "Thank you, Morgan."

WHEN SHE AWOKE, she was aware of him instantly. He was beside her, his muscled, rough leg entwined intimately with hers. She was on her side, and he was close behind her, like a spoon. His large hand was splayed over her breast, holding it gently. His other hand was between her thighs, warm against the smooth skin.

With a soft exhalation, Delia glanced at the bedside clock. Five twenty-three. It was still dark outside, and very still. She tried to move, but their bodies were entwined in such a way that she couldn't.

She moved back against him, trying to ease his

hand out from between her thighs, when she felt his strong arousal. Moving forward again, she pulled at his hand. Dead weight.

He shifted in his sleep, and his fingers pressed her more intimately. Delia started, then shifted. She'd have to wake him.

"Morgan?" she whispered.

"Hmm?" His voice was a soft rasp, still sleepy.

"Could you move your hand for just a second?"

He did, and she felt his fingers graze her hip before settling on her waist.

"Your other hand?"

He complied, moving it to her shoulder and giving it a soft squeeze.

Both touches had been soft, nonsexual. There was nothing Morgan had done that could have been interpreted as an overture to intimacy. Yet as his hand squeezed her shoulder, Delia knew she wanted him to make love to her.

It was unfair, manipulating him in a semiawake state, but she didn't think about it as she raised her thigh gently and reached between her legs to touch him intimately. She trailed her fingertips over the taut flesh, then grasped him more firmly. Shifting in front of him, she brought the tip of his masculinity to her most intimate place.

She felt his hand tighten at her waist; then it slid slowly, luxuriously, to the back of her thigh. He pushed lightly, and she raised her leg a bit

more. The springs protested softly as he shifted
his hips behind her and entered her just the tiniest bit.

She groaned at the exquisite sensation. His
hand moved again, and she felt his palm pressed
firmly against her abdomen, fingers apart. He
moved down until one of his fingers was tangled
in the soft curl of hair between her thighs. Then
slowly, unerringly, he found the spot he wanted
and began to move his fingertip over it, slowly.
So slowly.

She arched her hips back, bringing him more
fully inside her. He groaned, and she felt his
hand tighten slightly on her stomach. His other
hand caught her hair and pulled it slightly, easing
her head back so his lips could claim hers.

It was the most tender of kisses, his lips soft
and warm. She opened her mouth at the same
moment he thrust again, gently. She moaned
against his mouth, then turned her head away
and buried it in the pillow. It felt so good, so
right, to be this close to Morgan. She had wanted
this from the first moment she'd seen him on
her father's balcony. Not fast, frenzied lovemaking. But this. This slow sensuality. She wanted
Morgan to make her body sing with life, to catch
her up in a wheel of fire that would take her far
away from all the hurt and pain.

And she wanted him. More than any man
she'd ever known. She wanted him because she
loved him. She'd never stopped loving him. All
the times she'd sat in a darkened theater and
watched him, all the moments she'd stopped

and simply stared out into space and wondered where he was, what he was doing, how he was feeling—everything had led up to this moment. This closeness. This feeling of being one with him.

The feeling was the same, but different. She'd made love to him before, but in six years they'd become slightly different people. So it was a combination of old and new. And achingly tender.

She moved her hips back, suddenly hungry for all of him, but his fingers tightened on her stomach, then moved lower. She stopped. His mouth moved to her shoulder, and he bit it gently, sending shivers racing throughout her body. Though she had started their intimacy, he was going to finish it. She felt him move, his motions smooth and graceful as he positioned himself behind her. Then he thrust strongly, once, twice. She cried out, then bit down on her lip as pleasure became almost unbearable in its intensity.

He filled her completely, the sensation extremely satisfying. She felt his hand move back down, unerring as he found her again and began to slowly build her excitement. At the same time, his other hand moved underneath her body. She shifted slightly, then sighed as his fingers closed over one of her breasts, the soft, kneading caresses making her nipple pucker and harden.

He took his time, building passion until she thought she would float right out of her body and shatter. As a feeling of inevitability began to overtake her, she heard him whisper against her ear.

"Yes." His voice was still husky with sleep. "So good."

The sound of his voice touched off her response, and she strained against him as she reached her peak. He held her hard against him, and she felt her muscles contract around him, almost painfully. It was a violent culmination for both of them, and she gasped, drawing in huge breaths as her body shuddered and finally was still. She could feel his body trembling with the aftermath of their passion.

He kissed her shoulder, then moved back, still inside her but not touching her other than where their bodies were intimately joined. When Delia stopped trembling, she slowly looked over her shoulder at him and smiled. She knew her lips were shaking, but she couldn't help it.

He moved closer until their bodies touched completely, his front to her back. She heard his labored breathing close to her ear. After several minutes she eased apart from his strong arms, then cradled his head against her breasts. She slid her fingers gently against the damp skin on his back, over powerful muscles.

When he caught his breath, he raised his head and smiled down at her, then kissed the tip of her nose softly.

"So much for my good intentions," he murmured, nuzzling her ear, then kissing her neck. "God, you smell good."

She moved her body against his, delighting in the way they fit so closely together.

He cupped her buttocks and pulled her tightly against him, then gave her a gentle swat. "It was wonderful." He kissed her cheek. "You don't know how many evenings I've stayed awake in this bed, wishing you were here with me, making love."

"I've had the same dreams."

"It was better than I remembered," he said, grinning wickedly. He glanced over at the clock. "Didn't you say something about an eight o'clock shoot?"

She sat up in bed, looking for the dial. "Oh, my God. It's ten after seven!"

"Better get a move on." He got out of bed and stretched, and Delia had to take a second to admire his unsuspecting form. "You have your choice, Delia. A quick shower with me or breakfast."

"So who needs to eat?" she replied quickly, and was rewarded by the bright gleam of appreciation in his dark eyes.

THE NEXT WEEK PASSED quickly for Delia. Filming was coming along brilliantly; the chemistry between James and Morgan was perfect. Delia let them have their heads, and she knew as she looked through the camera lens that she was seeing film history in the making. Neither actor had ever been this outstanding in a role before.

If her days were filled with filmmaking, her nights were filled with lovemaking. It was an un-

spoken agreement between Morgan and herself.
No commitment had been made, but she moved
in a few of her clothes. He gave her one of the
drawers in his dresser. They spent evenings together at the house with James. Delia watched
the way her father would laugh as Morgan made
his early days in the London theater come alive.
And she knew he was remembering his rise to
fame, much the same way Morgan's career had
come about. The two men enjoyed each other
immensely, and Delia wished they had known
each other sooner in both their lives.

For a brief time James was filling the roll of
the father Morgan had never known; Morgan,
the son James had never had. There was laughter and warmth in their evenings together, and
Delia was content to sit back and watch the two
men dearest in the world to her enjoy each
other's company.

She loved watching them together. Many evenings, Morgan would ask James to get out the
videocassettes he had of his older films—Mary
had recorded them off the television. The two of
them would watch James's performances, and
Morgan would ask countless questions. Delia
watched as James patiently explained what he
thought had made a scene work, and why. And
she sensed her father's contentment. He was
passing something on to Morgan, and perhaps in
that sense, he wouldn't die.

Meals were filled with teasing and laughter.
Now that Morgan was cooperating on the set,
Delia was much more relaxed, could enjoy her

evenings more. The three of them watched the dailies together in the evenings, though Morgan hated to watch himself on film. But that was part of what James insisted made up a good actor, so Morgan relented. And Delia found their comments helpful as she made notes to herself to help with the final cutting of the film.

Her nights with Morgan were a world apart from any she had ever known. Even during their time together in London he had never pushed her as hard, made love to her as fiercely, demanded so much of her. She was stronger now, and she took everything he gave her and gave back again, until they both lay back in a tangle of sheets and could only look at each other, amazed.

One night, after they had satisfied their desire for each other and lay encompassed within the warm aftermath of their passion, Morgan broke the unspoken boundaries that had previously enabled them to resume their relationship without the complications of their past.

"What are you using?" he asked lazily as he caressed her back.

"Nothing you have to worry about," she said as she stroked the soft hair by his ear. She would never grow tired of touching him as long as she could just be with him.

"I want to worry about it. What are you using?"

She leaned up and whispered in his ear, then lay back in the warm circle of his arms.

"Do you feel good about it?"

She shrugged. "It's the best of a bunch of bad possibilities."

"Don't you want children?" As her head came back up and she looked down at him, he continued. "I've heard it's not the best method for a woman who still wants children. Unless you've already settled the question."

"I haven't settled it." She knew she was walking on very delicate ground. What exactly was Morgan asking her?

"You're twenty-eight now. When were you planning on settling it?" He sounded concerned.

"I always assumed that some man would come along," she answered frankly.

"Some man meaning besides me."

"Yes."

"Did some man ever come along?"

"Can I ask you the same question?"

"Certainly." His hand tightened slightly on her hip. "Ladies first."

"How many women did you sleep with after I left you?"

"Ouch." He rolled her on top of him, and she tried to concentrate on the question, not on the way his chest hairs tickled her breasts.

"Do you mind my bluntness?" she asked.

"I thought you might couch your question so I wouldn't have to be quite so specific."

"I don't want a score card. You don't have to tell me how many times with each woman."

"All right. Do you promise not to leave this bed if I tell you the truth?"

She swallowed. "Yes."

"Three."

"Three!"

"I'm sorry, Delia, but I'm not a monk!"

"I'm not mad. It's just— Only three, Morgan? Are you lying to me?"

"No."

"I don't believe you!"

He grasped her buttocks firmly with one hand, then rolled across the large bed so that she was pinned firmly beneath him. "I knew this discussion would get us in nothing but trouble."

"We're not in trouble! I just don't believe you!"

"Why not?"

"You've worked with some of the most beautiful women in the world—"

"Some of whom can be nothing but a bloody pain in the neck."

"But they must have come on to you!"

He kissed the side of her neck gently. "Oh, so now I'm irresistible, is that it?"

"I just—" She stopped talking as his mouth came down firmly over hers, then parted her lips, deepening the kiss until she forgot what they had been talking about.

"How many?" he said quietly.

"How many what?" She felt soft and languid. Shifting her hips beneath him, she pressed herself softly against his arousal.

"You're not going to get away with that little trick. I answered your question, so you have to

answer mine. How many men have you been—"
it seemed he could barely get the word out of his
mouth "—close to?"

"Do you really want to know?" She'd seen
doubt in his eyes, and she didn't want to hurt
him.

"Yes. Now that we've started, I have to
know."

"Two." At his frown, she put a quick finger to
his lips. "One right after— I was trying to erase
you—it was awful, Morgan. It took me a long
time to get up my courage after that. The second
time—I thought he was someone special. But he
never made me feel the way you did. We dated
for a while, but I broke it off. I thought he would
help me feel less lonely, but I felt—worse."

Tears started to gather in her eyes as she remembered the horrible feelings of emptiness that
had followed each encounter. Morgan gently
bent his head and kissed her cheek, stopping the
tear as it slid down her face.

"I thought of you." He sighed. "I thought of
you every time I laid a hand on another woman.
I made love with one of the women because she
had a smile that looked a lot like yours. I wasn't
terribly proud of myself."

"Was she pretty?" She couldn't stop the
questions.

"Not as pretty as you," he whispered softly.

"Did she love you?"

"No. Not especially. We both knew what we
were getting into."

"Did you love her?"

"That's a foolish question." He kissed her again, and his hand moved gently to her breast. "There's only one woman I've ever loved, and she's right in bed beside me."

"You love me?"

"Always. I never stopped."

She looked at him for several long seconds, wanting to remember every detail of this moment. The way the bedside lamp cast a soft glow over the small, wood-paneled room. The gentle pressure of his body against hers. The scent of his body, the feel of his long fingers as they gently caressed her breast. His eyes were dark and vulnerable, his expression open at last. No matter what kind of an actor he was, Morgan couldn't fake this. It felt too right.

"What are you thinking?" she asked, running her fingers over his smooth back, to the muscles of his thighs.

"I'm thinking," he said slowly as he leaned over and turned off the bedside lamp, "that we have a lot of lost time to make up for."

Chapter Seven

"We haven't seen you in a long time," Tom said as Delia walked into the stable.

"Just too busy with production details," she teased. It was the first morning in over a week she hadn't stayed in bed with Morgan as late as possible. Mary knew she rarely showed up for breakfast, but, like Tom, she was too discreet a person to ask questions. Delia knew both Tom and Mary were simply happy that she no longer looked as tense and worried as before.

She tried to keep her voice casual. "Morgan will be riding with me this morning, so would it be okay if I saddled up Pogo or King Arthur for him?"

Fifteen minutes later, up on Cinderina's back, with Morgan beside her on trusty Pogo, a chubby pinto, Delia took delight in showing him the ranch.

The mountains were clearly visible today, not hidden in the clouds. Delia decided to take Morgan to one of the small creeks that ran through the property. It was an offshoot of the Gros

Ventre River, and as the weather was some-where in the eighties and the sun was beating down on both of them, she decided that sitting by a creek would be a cool way to pass the after-noon.

It was silent as they rode. The only sounds were an occasional snort from one of the horses and the gentle squeak of saddle leather. Delia was comfortable in the silence. Since Morgan had told her so much about his feelings during the dinner they had shared in Jackson, she wanted him to understand her feelings about the ranch. It was an area of extremes, both in climate and sheer natural beauty. It spoke to something deep inside Delia, and she realized as she rode by Morgan's side that she'd come to love this land as much as James did. It fed the soul.

"It's immense. I didn't think there would be this much land," Morgan said later as they sat by the creek. Both Pogo and Cinderina grazed nearby, while Delia and Morgan sat underneath a tree, enjoying the picnic Delia had persuaded Mary to pack for them. Delia firmly believed that people worked better after a day off.

They lay in the sun, Delia in faded jeans and a bright red tank top, Morgan in jeans and a white T-shirt with "Drinkin' at the Lincoln Bar and Grill" slashed across it in bright blue let-ters.

"You're going to burn your nose," he in-formed her, tapping it with his finger.

She leaned against him, the sun warming his T-shirt. Rummaging through the large canvas bag she'd brought with them, she took out a tube of sunscreen and began to rub some of the ointment on her face.

"Would you put some on my arms? I always burn." His voice sounded disarmingly innocent.

"You're browner than Pogo's patches," she informed him nonchalantly, but she rubbed some of the sunscreen into his muscular arms, enjoying the feel of his skin underneath her fingers.

"You do that so well."

"I'm at your service," she teased as she took a cloth out of the large picnic basket and spread it out over one of the large, flat rocks by the riverbed.

"What did Mary make today? She's one hell of a talented cook. I'm having trouble keeping my weight down."

"We can't have that. Desperadoes in the Old West never had paunches."

"I can hold in my stomach with the best of them. Do I see chocolate cake?"

"You do," she informed him as she placed the chocolate confection out of his reach, "but you have to eat the main course first."

She pulled out more of Mary's fried chicken, a marinated vegetable dish, fresh peaches and a bottle of champagne.

Morgan's voice was dry. "Somehow I can't picture Mary packing us a bottle of champagne."

"She didn't. I raided the fridge."

"Don't tell me I have to eat everything before I get some champagne.'

"You don't. You just have to open it for me."

He took the corkscrew she handed him and opened the bottle carefully, while Delia extracted two crystal champagne glasses and some fresh strawberries.

"You brought those glasses on horseback?"

"I told you Cinderina's gait was smooth."

"You're really something."

She filled each glass to the brim. The champagne sparkled in the strong, bright sunlight, the strawberries bobbing amid bubbles.

"What's the occasion?" Morgan asked.

She raised the fragile glass. "To us. To being back together again. I wanted to tell you—" her voice grew lower, and she leaned closer "—I adore you. I have no intention of letting go a second time around."

"Did I ever tell you the feeling is mutual?"

She laughed, feeling younger than she had in years. "To us." She tilted her glass up and took a quick sip of champagne.

"Am I going to have to carry you home?" Morgan sounded as if the prospect were pleasurable.

"Not just yet. I thought you might want to ravish me in the fields first. After the ravishing, then you can carry me."

"A woman after my own heart. You'll have to feed me first before I can gather up the strength to ravish you. The hours you've put me through over the past few nights—"

"Me! You're the one who always wants to make love again! I'm all ready to call it an evening, but you always give me one more little nudge—"

"And you resist so well." He could barely keep the laughter out of his voice.

It was an afternoon filled with teasing banter and love. Delia knew the only time she'd ever been happier with Morgan was when they had taken one of their trips to Italy. She loved the feeling of being alone with him, not having any pressing worries for the moment. Filming was tomorrow. When she had left the house that morning, James and Mary had been out on the back porch watching the sun rise. James had looked peaceful. It was a rare day, and Delia, more conscious of the preciousness of life, responded to the moment.

I'm glad Dad is alone with Mary. They needed the time together. For whatever private reasons, James and Mary had never had children of their own, instead focusing all their love and affection on Delia and their horses. She knew James's death would be horrible for Mary. Living together for twenty-two years had to create a bond hard to break. And because they'd remained childless, except for summers when she visited, they were that much closer.

"What are you thinking about?" Morgan's soft voice brought her out of her thoughts.

She decided to concentrate on the man she was with. "How much I enjoy you this way. How I hope nothing ever comes between us again."

He sighed, then took her hand and placed it on his chest. Stretching out, he lay down on the

ground next to the remains of their picnic. "I
hope so. This time nothing is going to go
wrong."

They lay in the sun for a long time. It was
pleasant, lying next to Morgan, her hand on his
chest, over his heart. She moved her fingers
gently over his smooth muscles and was rewarded when she felt his heartbeat speed up
slightly.

"You're playing with fire," Morgan said, his
eyes closed.

Delia sat up and brushed a bead of perspiration away from her forehead. "How would you
feel about going for a swim?"

"Where?"

"There's a place not far from here where
some rocks dam up the creek. It's not too deep,
and the water's terrific."

"Sounds good." He grinned, and Delia felt
her heart turn over as she saw the lazily erotic
look in his eyes. "What are you planning on using as a suit?"

She gave him a quick kiss on his nose. "My
birthday suit."

"This does promise to be interesting."

They packed up all their picnic supplies, careful not to leave any litter to mar the surroundings. Then, swinging up in the saddle, Delia
called back, "Follow me!"

She ran Cinderina at an easy canter, careful of
the fact that both she and Morgan couldn't risk a
fall. The creek wasn't far away, and soon they
were dismounting by the banks, letting the reins

of the horses fall over their heads as a signal to stay.

Delia shed her clothes quickly. She'd always loved to swim in the nude; there was nothing else that inspired such a wild pagan feeling. Almost nothing else, she thought as she watched Morgan pull his T-shirt over his head, exposing smooth bronze muscles.

Stepping out of her jeans, she dropped them on one of the warm rocks and ran down to the creek's edge, feeling very young and carefree and gloriously alive. "Come on, Morgan. Race you in!"

She ran to where she knew the water was deep and sprang in, feet first. Ice-cold water closed over her head, shocking her body into glorious awareness. Kicking strongly, she surfaced, arching her head back so that her hair was swept cleanly off her face. Laughing, she looked toward the bank.

Morgan was standing on the same rock she had dove off, looking down into the clean, deep water.

"Is it cold?" he asked.

She laughed. "Don't be a baby! It's warm as tea! Come on in." She crossed her fingers underneath the water. The creek was fed from a mountain stream, so even though the weather was warm, the depths of the water were still frigid.

She started to laugh again as he dove in and was convulsed with giggles as he shot to the surface, roaring his indignity.

"You little liar! It's cold as hell!" She was still laughing as he began to swim toward her with strong, powerful strokes. Grabbing her around the waist, they both tread water.

"That was a sneaky move," Morgan said. But he didn't sound mad.

She was still laughing, little hiccuping sounds that made her body shimmer against his. "It was the only way I could think of," she said, reaching down to touch him intimately, "that we could be close together and not end up making love." At the look of incredulity on his face, she was sent into another wave of laughter.

"So you don't like it, huh?" He threaded his fingers into her hair and bent her head back.

"Morgan, not in the water!"

He kicked strongly, keeping them both above water. Then, grabbing her underneath her arms, he rolled over on his back and began to swim toward shore.

"You know," she said, trying not to laugh, "I read somewhere that Paul Newman used to dunk his head into a sink filled with ice cubes every morning to keep the skin on his face taut."

"So you thought I needed a treatment all over my body. Is that it?"

She started to laugh again. "Think how fresh you'll look in front of the camera tomorrow."

"I think I'm fresh enough." He was touching bottom now, and he pulled her to her feet. They both started walking toward the shore.

"There's a big rock up there that's perfect for sunbathing," she said, trying not to respond to the feel of his hands against her bare flesh. A part of her wanted to make him work at seducing her.

"Is it private?"

"I don't think anyone else is going to be riding out this way."

"Is it private enough for what I have in mind?"

"And what is that?"

Without warning, he slung her up over his shoulders and strode swiftly to the outcropping of flat rocks. Easing her down gently, he took one of her wrists in either hand and pressed them gently against the smooth, hot stone.

"I think you're going to have to pay for what you did back there," he said softly.

She started to playact, wriggling in his grasp. "Not the whip! Anything but the whip!"

"Anything?" He leaned over and kissed her collarbone, then the soft curves of her breasts. Moving his lips slowly down her body, he took one of her nipples into his mouth and tugged gently on it.

Delia sighed as she felt sexual feeling flow through her, as hot and smooth as a river of melted honey. She closed her eyes against the brightness of the sun, and all she could feel was his mouth on her body, teasing her, urging her into sensual bliss.

He kissed her for a long time, holding her wrists firmly, making it impossible for her to reciprocate. And it was exciting, being held in his firm grasp, not being able to respond except to pure sensation. He brought her hands down to her sides as he kissed her stomach, flicking his tongue into her navel, gently biting the sides of her hips. She moaned softly, loving the feelings he was evoking deep within her most intimate places.

When his lips moved to her inner thighs, she parted them obediently, not even thinking of denying him anything. She felt he was possessing her, leaving his mark. He'd already spoiled her for any other man, having awakened her to levels of ecstasy she'd never suspected existed. He loved her intimately, with lips and tongue. And when he let go of one of her wrists and used his skilled fingers to begin to touch her, her hand trembled. It seemed impossible so much feeling, such emotion, could be contained by her body. Moving her fingers slowly, she touched his hair and blindly caressed his cheek.

By the time he levered his body over hers, she was arching her hips gently, wanting him deep inside, wanting him to finish their loving. Desiring a closeness, a feeling of completeness. Lowering his mouth over hers, he kissed her, his tongue slipping inside her mouth to tantalize her with erotic movements. In and out, he caressed her mouth, at the same time rubbing his hot, aroused flesh against the smooth skin of her stomach. When his lips left hers, she gasped, her breath weak. He was the only man who could bring her so quickly, so effortlessly, to this mindless state.

"Please."

"Mmm." His mouth closed over one of her breasts.

"Please, Morgan."

"Please what?"

"Please love me—" She reached down for him, closed her fingers over the proud, hot flesh and squeezed gently.

Their joining was intense, passionate. Possessive. Morgan made love to her as if she were about to leave him. There was something poignant in the way he touched her face, kissed her, gave her pleasure.

Afterward, lying very still in the sun, they faced each other, her head on his shoulder, his hand on her thigh.

"You're mine, Delia," he said, so softly that if she hadn't been listening, she wouldn't heave heard him.

She nodded, her head still against his shoulder. And she knew what had happened today was exactly what she had been afraid of the night she'd first seen him on the balcony. Morgan wasn't a man to do anything halfway.

But she was still frightened by what lay ahead.

LATER THAT EVENING, Delia wandered out by the stable to watch Tom work with Hades. He had the horse on a longe line, and the black stallion was trotting obediently around the corral.

Delia leaned her arms against the rail, enjoying the sight. The animal had come a long way in only a matter of weeks. Tom had a special perception when it came to horses, and it was obviously serving him well with the stallion.

After the training session was over, he unsnapped the longe line from Hades' hackamore and gave the stallion a light pat on the rump. The dark horse snorted, kicked up his heels lightly and galloped to the far end of the corral.

"You're amazing," Delia called to him.

Tom took off his hat and wiped his sleeve across his brow. "I could say the same for you, miss. I've never seen your Mister Buckmaster in a better temper."

She laughed delightedly. "Tom!"

He crossed the distance between them quickly, then climbed over the fence with sure, agile movements. Standing next to Delia, he searched in the pocket of his denim jacket for a cigarette and a match.

Cupping his hands against the evening breeze, Tom lit the cigarette, then snuffed out the match and lay it carefully on the rail. Delia knew he would put it in the pocket of his jacket before he left. Tom, like the rest of them at the ranch, abhorred litter of any kind.

"James looks good, doesn't he?" Delia murmured almost to herself as she looked at the mountains in the distance. The sun was just setting, tinting the granite faces with hues of pink and lavender and a touch of gold.

"They always look good right before they go."

"No, Tom—" She turned away from him, tensing her body against the rush of emotion threatening to consume her.

She felt his hands on her shoulders, warm and steadying. "You've got to face it, Delia. You can give the old man immortality on film, but it's his time, and he knows it."

"I know—"

"You know here." He touched his head lightly. "But not here," he said, putting his hand over his heart.

"I can't imagine him gone."

"Neither can I." Tom took a deep drag on his cigarette, then expelled the smoke into the deepening twilight. "I don't know who I'll argue with."

Tom took another drag, then squinted his eyes against the smoke as he blew it back out.

"Will you—will you stay after he's gone?" Delia's voice was thick with unshed tears.

"Now where else would I go, miss? Someone has to look out for Mary, and you're going to have to go back to California and finish up the film."

They leaned on the railing, enjoying the comfortable silence of two old friends.

"I remember the first summer you came out here. As horse crazy as all get-out. Do you remember the time you decided to give that dappled pony a bath?"

Delia started to laugh. She knew Tom was deliberately trying to lighten the conversation, and she went along. "I remember when you and Dad came out into the corral and saw all the mud!"

"And when you read that story about the animals talking on Christmas Eve, so you crept out to the barn and caused quite an uproar when no one could find you."

"And when Cinderina had her little filly. Remember how scared we were and the way Dad insisted someone stay with her all the time. And when Valentina took the ribbon in the barrel-racing contest?"

"You were so sick from all the junk you ate, Mary had to take you back to the hotel room."

They were silent for a moment longer; then Tom said softly, "We had good times, Delia. Nothing can ever take away your memories." He took one of her hands in his, and she felt the leathery quality of his palm against hers. "I want you to remember something for me, miss."

"Anything."

"When he goes—and he will—it's going to tear you apart. Nothing will ever be the same, and you'll never get over it. Don't listen to the people who say time heals. You always remember. You'll think of James when you see things he would have liked, when you notice things that remind you of him. There will never be a man who will replace him in that special part of your heart."

She bowed her head on the arm still remaining on the rail. Everything Tom said had to be said. It was so hard to face.

"But he won't be dead where it matters—in your heart and in your mind. You can always close your eyes and remember how he looked when he was bellowing about something. Or think of a funny time or remember how much he loved you."

She couldn't say anything.

Tom hugged her against him fiercely. "I told the old man I'd look after you, so if you ever need to talk about anything, come to me."

"Tom—" Her voice was breaking.

"It will hurt like hell. But we'll have to think of Mary, and we'll have to go on. I thank you for giving James the picture. I wanted to see him go out with a roar. I love that man. I've talked with God every night since I found out about the cancer. I don't understand it, and I won't pretend to. I don't want to hear anyone say it's for the best or it's God's will. James Wilde was kind to me when I needed help. He remembered me, and he helped me. There aren't many men in the world like that. You remember that, miss, and be proud you had such a fine da."

Delia bent her knees slightly and gave Tom a fierce hug. She wasn't surprised to find his cheek as wet as hers.

"QUIET!" Delia's voice was low, but it carried perfectly. The set was closed today; only the minimum number of crew were present. Today was the scene the entire film rested upon: James's confrontation with Morgan.

She had tried to film the scene on Monday and Tuesday, but Mary had forewarned her that James wasn't feeling well. So Delia had juggled her scenes and ended up directing Morgan and Belinda. Morgan probably thought she was disorganized, but he didn't say a word. But today James felt better, and Delia knew what Tom had said Sunday evening at the corral was true: it was almost time.

"Okay, whenever the two of you are ready." She addressed her comment to James and Morgan, both standing by the split-rail fence surrounding one of the smaller cabins on the property. This was supposed to be the cabin shared by Mary Anne and her father. Morgan, as Mary Anne's lover, was coming to take her away from her father. It was James's one long monologue, and Delia silently prayed he would find the strength to carry it through.

James and Morgan looked at each other for a second; then Morgan nodded his head slightly. Delia picked up the signal immediately, and she nodded toward Charlie. The cameras began to roll.

Delia willed herself to remain calm, but her nails were biting into her palms. *Please, let him be able to do the scene.* She had already looked through the lens. The weather was perfect, early summer in all its glory. The sky was so blue it almost hurt to look at it, and there wasn't a cloud in sight. The wind was gentle, the sun not as hot as it had been earlier in filming.

She could hear Morgan delivering his lines angrily, letting James know he was going to take Belinda whether he wanted him to or not. Morgan caught fire every time he shared a scene with James, and he was doing brilliantly today, his gestures spontaneous, his actions perfectly natural. When you watched Morgan act, you forgot he was playing a part.

Delia knew the script by heart, and she found herself mouthing the lines along with Morgan. Closer, closer—

"No!" It was a cry of pure anguish, from the deepest recesses of James's soul. Morgan stopped, and the stunned look on his face was perfect. He was reacting to James, to what was happening right now. Delia had been with them when they'd run their lines this morning, but James had saved his intensity until now. Morgan was clearly stunned, but his instinctive reaction was absolutely right.

"No." James's voice was quieter now, more resigned. He looked at Morgan for a long moment, and Delia held her breath. *Now.*

"She's all I have," James said quietly, looking down at his hands, which trembled slightly. Delia knew it was from pain, but it was also perfect within the context of the script.

Morgan found his next line, and the simple intensity he gave it matched James beautifully. "But I love her. I—"

"You don't understand." James's eyes blazed now, and with superhuman effort he pulled himself upright and looked down at Morgan. "You've taken everything I own and destroyed it. You took the land and water for your people. You stole my cattle, tried to burn my barn. And you want to take my daughter!" He was roaring now, and Delia knew with a deep certainty that the film being created would blaze with the fire that was uniquely James Wilde's.

"She loves me," Morgan said defiantly, and

Delia realized how perfectly matched they were, a king and a dark prince.

"You earn love like that. You don't just take it."

"She'll come to me! You can't keep her tied to you forever!" Morgan was perfect, arrogant and proud.

"Yes, she will." James gripped the railing tightly, then looked out over the meadow toward the mountains. There was a peculiar expression on his face, a timeless certainty. "But you won't ask her."

"The hell I won't—"

"You won't ask her because I won't be keeping her much longer. Can't you give me that, man? Do I have to go down on my knees and beg?" There was anguish in his dark blue eyes, and Delia didn't even raise her hand to wipe the tears that were beginning to slip silently down her cheeks.

He was wonderful.

"I won't keep her much longer, because I don't have much longer! You know that as well as I do! For God's sake, let me keep her here until summer's end! You can have her after that. But I want that much time!"

Morgan was very still, waiting.

James's voice was tight with emotion. "I've never asked anyone for anything. I've worked for everything in my life, and the only good thing is Mary Anne. You'll have her for a life-time—give me a few more weeks." He wasn't begging, he was willing Morgan's character to do his bidding. Delia watched, fascinated, the change come over Morgan's face.

"And if I do?"

"Then she's yours. She loves you. I know that. I've watched her face when she looks at you. She loved you from the very first moment, and love like that doesn't come often. But when it does, it's worth every bit of pain. I loved her mother like that, and those were the happiest years of my life. What's all this—" as he spoke, James made a sweeping gesture that encompassed everything around him, the land and sky and trees "—when you don't have someone to talk to. To laugh with. My Mary Anne, she's a laugher. And a talker. You think she's gentle, but she's strong when she has to be. I don't have any right to ask you this, but I want you to take care of her. I want you to always be there when she needs you. Don't ever take my daughter for granted. If you love her the way she should be loved, you'll have something so rich you won't have to fight for the land. You'll have everything a man could want right in the palm of your hand."

Without a word, Morgan nodded, then turned slowly and walked toward his horse. He mounted smoothly, lifted the reins and turned the animal, then pressed his heels against its sides and galloped away.

James watched him from the fence until he rounded a bend of trees and disappeared from sight.

"Cut. That's it." When the cameras stopped rolling, Delia ran to her father.

"Dad, that was—"

"I'm tired, Delia. Could you walk me to the trailer?"

She held his hand tightly and put her arm around his shoulder as she led him toward one of the trailers they'd set up on the edge of the clearing. He was leaning so much of his weight on her that she stumbled once, but she regained her footing quickly and concentrated on putting one foot in front of the other. No one seemed to notice, and Morgan still had to bring the horse back. Delia kept her eyes trained on their destination as she supported her father. Where was Tom?

The few steps leading up to the inside of the trailer were hard to negotiate, but once inside, James lay down, and Delia ran to the small refrigerator and poured him a glass of water.

"Drink this." For the first time in her father's long illness, she was scared.

She helped him sit up and guided the water to his lips. He held her arm as he drank.

The soft knock on the door stopped her thoughts, and she eased James back slowly on the small bed. Taking the glass and setting it in the sink, she answered the door.

Morgan stood there, a look of concern on his face. "Is James all right? He seemed—"

"He's tired." Delia automatically closed the circle of protection closely around her father. She didn't want any rumors escaping, didn't want anything to harm the film. She was almost finished, and then she could devote full time to James.

"Is there anything I can do?"

She was about to say no when he continued, a note of care in his low voice.

"Please, Delia, don't shut me out."

Did he know? Delia decided to share as much as she could. "He's getting old, and— Morgan, he can't give over all that energy and not feel the strain. Not at his age." She was thankful James couldn't hear her, or he might fly into a disagreement. Her father hated nothing more than arbitrary labeling, and he considered references to his age just that.

"Tell me how I can help you."

She hesitated for an instant, then decided he'd earned at least some of her trust. "Find Tom. Bring him here. Ask him to drive the truck as close as he can."

Without another word he vanished around the side of the trailer.

And Delia went back to her father and lay her fingers against his cheek. The skin was thin, his color bad. The beginnings of an understanding of what was going to happen to him ripped through her body, searing her with a pain so intense she didn't move.

MORGAN LAY QUIETLY in the darkness of his bedroom, his arms behind his head. He felt as if pieces were falling into place just beyond his grasp. His emotions boiled inside, and he was ashamed of them.

Why hadn't he realized he was still jealous of the relationship Delia had with her father? They were so close. He had seen her help him up the stairs, seen the way he'd leaned on her. She had accepted it, helped him, supported him. The perfect image for a very special kind of love.

He kept his eyes open in the darkness, because he knew if he closed them, he would remember all the pain.

He hadn't told Delia everything about his past. She knew he had no family, knew his mother had died when he was two. He could barely remember her. His father had died before he was born, and there had been no relatives. Or else none had wanted him.

He'd made light of the years he'd spent in the orphanage, because he honestly didn't know how to describe them. No one would believe. Understaffed and overcrowded, it had been a frightening place. He had started to build a fantasy life in his head at a very early age. It was the only beauty in his life. The only way he could survive.

One of the nuns had insisted the children be exposed to culture, so the local high school had been called in to perform a play. Morgan could still remember the feeling that had swept over him when he realized dreams could take on substance and form and become real. At the age of eleven he'd decided to become an actor.

He'd been a rebellious child and had endured many punishments. The hidden scars were still with him. But the deep wellspring of intense life that was such a part of him couldn't be suppressed.

At twelve he'd discovered the opposite sex. At fourteen he'd been initiated into love by a headstrong sixteen-year-old. He'd loved it, loved the feeling of being touched without being punished. To be held in a woman's arms in exchange for giving her pleasure was one of the great wonders of the universe to the boy he'd been.

He'd run away at sixteen. Looking older than his age, he'd hitched up the coast from San Diego and found work in Los Angeles. He'd made friends, drank, partied. He'd probably still be wasting his life away if it hadn't been for Randy.

Randy had wanted to be an actor. He'd asked Morgan to accompany him to an open audition. Once in sight of the stage, all the old dreams had returned. Perhaps because he'd had absolutely nothing to fall back on, Morgan felt he had nothing to lose.

He could still remember being called up onto the stage. He had said his lines loudly, with spirit. He'd taken the stage, scared of no one, terrified inside. And they called him back.

From bit parts to two television series, he'd worked hard and learned by experience. Then, burned out totally at the age of twenty-five, he dropped out of everything for six long months.

He had just enough money to spend some time thinking. And he didn't like the direction his life was taking. He had no close friends and spent most of his evenings partying with people he didn't like.

It was time to escape and reevaluate.

Morgan smiled tightly as he remembered his

agent's disbelief when he'd called and told the man he was leaving for London. He was going to learn what being a real actor was about. He was going to come back and take the world by storm.

His agent had laughed, then thrown another series in his face. This time, Morgan was to play a jaded lifeguard. At that moment, he'd looked at his future, long and hard.

He left for London within a week.

He'd lived by his instincts when he'd left the relative safety of the orphanage, and he used those instincts when he'd arrived in England. Within a few months he'd auditioned and been accepted at the academy.

There was a brief spate of publicity in the papers. California pretty boy goes to London to become an actor. Morgan, used to ignoring what he didn't want to see, simply continued his studies and didn't read the papers. Eventually, they turned to other news makers.

Then Delia had entered his life.

He smiled and relaxed back against the soft mattress. He could still remember the first time he'd seen her. In exercise class. Dressed in worn sweats, dripping with perspiration, he'd looked up in the mirror and seen her come in, drop her oversized canvas bag by the piano and lean against the wall, watching. She'd been on a tour of the classes, deciding whether she wanted to enroll.

He had missed a step in the routine he started every day with. The attraction had been that strong.

She'd been jumped into the advanced scene class because of her college work. He'd walked up to her the first day and asked her to do a scene with him. Romeo and Juliet. The balcony scene.

He'd wanted to kiss her.

The first time he kissed her, in rehearsal, she trembled. Onstage, she gave her all, and it was tremendously exciting. He asked her to a movie that same week. On their third date, she asked him up for coffee. At twenty, she'd been fresh and innocent. She reminded him of the deer he'd seen at the London zoo.

He cared for her so much it terrified him.

They dated for six months before he did anything but kiss her good-night. He avoided touching her at first, feeling instinctively that once started he wouldn't be able to stop. He'd been right.

On her twenty-first birthday he took her out to dinner at a local pub. He hadn't been ashamed of his lack of money yet. Delia had worn what everyone else wore; jeans and T-shirts, sweats and pullover sweaters. Functional clothing. He'd had no idea she was James Wilde's daughter.

Afterward, they'd walked around London and spun their dreams together. He loved her because he could share his deepest secrets with her and she listened. She knew what it was to be scared, unsure. To want something so badly and find it just beyond your reach.

He'd brought her home as usual, and she'd

asked him up. She'd made coffee and brought it to the living room.

And then she'd asked him why he wasn't attracted to her. He could still remember her face, earnest and distressed.

"I'm attracted to you. Too much." He set down his coffee cup and picked up his jacket.

"Why do you avoid touching me?" Her eyes were huge and hurt, dominating her entire face.

"You're too gentle, too naive—"

"Maybe I don't want to be naive any longer. And I'm not that gentle underneath."

"We're light-years apart, you and I."

"I love you!"

He'd admired her courage, her willingness to be honest about her deepest feelings. He could talk to her about anything but the way he felt about her.

"You don't know what love is about!"

"I do!" She stuck her chin out defiantly. "It's not as if I'm a virgin or something!"

He'd been amazed by her boldness. And aroused. But he'd left her that night, shut the door firmly behind him even though he heard her crying inside.

The next day she'd approached him with a scene. Romeo and Juliet. Their wedding night.

She'd wanted to sleep with him.

. The scene was brilliant. Their instructor had thought it admirable to continue studying the same play. By the end of two weeks of rehearsal, he was crazy to take her to bed. They walked out of class after performing the scene and went straight back to her flat, skipping vocal instruction.

She'd never been with a man before.

There were little signs that should have tipped him off, but he'd been so hot and eager, so ready. His hands shook as he touched her breasts, as he kissed her, pressing himself tightly against her naked body. Her skin was so smooth, so warm. Her arms so graceful. His eyes had almost filled with tears as she touched his cheek with a kind of wonder.

Even though he was gentle, she cried out when he took her. He'd stopped, but she'd held him tightly, moved beneath him until he couldn't think and simply made love to her. He'd never forget the look on her face.

She'd slowly opened her eyes and looked at him with the most pleased expression.

"I wanted you to be the first," she whispered.

He felt like a fool.

"You still don't know half of it," he answered softly.

"Will you teach me?" As she spoke, she touched his face gently. He was almost ashamed at his instant arousal.

He'd never left. Within a week, he'd moved all his things in. They lived together for eight months before he discovered she was James Wilde's daughter.

The neighbor downstairs had pounded on her ceiling with a broom handle, the fighting had been so intense.

"When the hell were you going to tell me?" he roared, furious with her and himself. How had he ever been stupid enough to believe she could be really his? He'd been thinking about asking her to marry him. Now it was out of the question.

"I didn't want to be different! I wanted to be—"

"Don't you ever lie to me again," he said, grasping her arms tightly. He'd left the apartment in a grand rage and gone out and gotten dead drunk. When he came back two days later, he had a plan.

He'd marry her. After he made a success of his career.

From that point on everything had gone into his acting. He pushed himself like the devil was riding him, working in two different plays at a time, going to parties to meet important industry people with a furious dedication.

And it was at that exact point that his relationship with Delia started to come apart.

Chapter Eight

"Morgan?"

The sound of Delia's voice brought him out of his thoughts of the past. He rolled over in bed and turned on the lamp.

"Why were you lying here in the dark?"

He knew her cheerfulness was a facade. Her smile didn't quite reach her eyes. She looked tired. Something was wrong, but he didn't know what.

"Just thinking."

About what?"

"Remembering. Do you remember when you were my Juliet?" He knew he could talk her out of her mood.

"I was scared to death when you asked me."

"I was scared asking. Do you know the first time I saw you, I felt as if someone had punched me in the stomach?"

"When was that?"

He could tell she was pleased. "You came walking into the exercise class, cool as you please. I took one look in the mirror and almost fell over."

"I don't remember that. I remember seeing the class, but I don't remember you."

He laughed. "It's better you didn't. I wasn't at my best."

"The first time I saw you—" she sat down on the bed and kicked off her boots, then curled up next to him "—was when I was jumped to the advanced class. I was terrified, but when I looked at you, you smiled at me. It made me feel warm inside, like I already knew you."

"And what things I had planned for you!" He hugged her tightly against him, wishing she would tell him what was really on her mind.

"You were always so careful with me."

"With good reason. You know what I loved most?"

"What?" she asked.

"Our walks. Do you remember the night we stayed out until almost five, walking around Picadilly Circus?"

"And you bought me that little stuffed dog."

"And we had to be up for class at eight. Everyone thought we were sleeping together, because we both looked like hell the next morning."

Delia smiled, then turned her cheek so it rested on his bare shoulders. "I didn't mind. Most of the girls were jealous."

"You look tired." He decided to change the subject, hoping it would be the opening she needed. But he saw her hesitation and knew what she was going to say wasn't what he wanted to hear.

"I was worried about the scene today. It's

pivotal. But it went like a dream. You were marvelous, the way you reacted to my father.''

He didn't want to talk about her father. Morgan wanted to know what was bothering her. There was something beyond the picture at stake here, and he wanted to know what he was up against.

"He really knows how to approach a scene. How is he feeling about it?"

She closed her eyes. "I think he loved being out there today. He enjoys working with you so much, Morgan. Thank you for staying."

"I was an ass." His fingers touched her neck softly, then her jaw, gently turning her head so he could see her eyes. "You're a very good director, Delia Wilde."

She seemed touched by his openhearted admission. "It's the people I'm working with. You're all terrific. You and Belinda and James—"

Morgan shook his head. "But you make us feel safe, and you give us ideas. The atmosphere around this film is very different from what I've been used to. It's as if—I feel like I can take more chances. You know how important that is for an actor."

She nodded. "Do you really think so?"

"I know how I feel. I enjoy working with you. I'm sorry for everything I said before."

"It's all right."

They lay silently on the bed for several moments; then Delia whispered in his ear, "Do you want to make love?"

"You're dead on your feet. It couldn't be that much fun for you."

She smiled sleepily, without opening her eyes. "I could just lie here, and you could—"

"Very funny!" He kissed her on the cheek, then got up off the bed. Pulling the quilt back, he eased her underneath. Morgan took off his clothes, then slid underneath the covers and helped Delia undress. When she was naked, he turned off the light and moved next to her, enfolding her in his arms very carefully.

She still hadn't told him.

MUCH LATER IN THE EVENING, he couldn't sleep. Thoughts tormented him. He lay in bed and listened to Delia's even breathing. The warmth and scent of her body were comforting to him.

He'd make her tell him. Was there another man in her life? She'd said no, but six years was a long time. Was she having second thoughts about their relationship starting up again? Was it going to continue after filming came to an end? He knew he wanted it to.

He could still remember their last argument as if it had happened only a few days ago. There weren't too many scenes from his earlier life he cared to remember. But that was one.

They had both tried hard to salvage their relationship, but knowing who Delia really was and the type of life she was used to had done something irrevocable to his feelings. He still loved her. It had been agony thinking about living without her. Yet he was haunted by feelings of inadequacy. How could he, an orphan of the state and streets, hope to deserve one of the film world's royalty?

And so he had watched the steady deterioration of their love. He had seen it in her eyes, in the hurt expression she had when she didn't know he was looking at her. She had tried so hard, it had been painful to watch. He hadn't given her anything back, had simply worked himself into the ground, after the damn money and the longed-for career. The proof of his worth.

They had stayed together for six months after that. But on the evening of their last argument he'd stumbled into the apartment, so tired he could barely see. His plan was working. He'd been tentatively accepted for a film, and the script was superior to anything he'd ever done before. There was no contract yet, but if all went well tonight— If he made even a modest amount of money, he would feel all right about asking her to marry him.

She'd met him at the door, looking desperate and confused. For just an instant he'd wanted to pull her into his arms. But they couldn't go backward in their relationship—not after he'd found out.

"You were supposed to be home at six," she informed him tightly. The apartment smelled of basil and garlic. Fresh pesto sauce. It was a good sign.

"I met a man—"

"I'm so sick of all the people you've met,"

she said, turning away and walking over toward the window.

"I'm doing it for you!" His temper flared, always close to the surface when he was tired.

"I don't care! I never see you anymore! When we decided to live together, it was so we could see each other all the time!"

"That was before—"

"God, don't start that. That was before you found out who I was, and I still don't understand why it had to change anything!"

He walked out of the living room and into the kitchen to get something to drink. As he opened the refrigerator door, he saw the pieces of pasta stuck against the wall. Looking down, he understood. Pieces of ceramic and what was supposed to have been dinner were all over one end of the kitchen. The bread had been flung on top of it; the bottle of wine was unopened on the small counter space.

He knew he was behaving badly, but he wanted to goad her. Couldn't she at least appreciate how hard he was working? Walking back out into the kitchen, he said quietly, "What's for dinner?"

"Nothing."

"Am I supposed to eat it off the floor?"

"If you want to."

"Why did you throw it?"

"I burned my hand."

He forgot his anger. Crossing the room, he took her hand and turned the palm upward. She jerked it away.

"Oh, for God's sake, Morgan, don't pretend!"

"What are you talking about?"

"I'm not stupid! Give me some credit for a little intelligence!"

"Will you tell me what—"

"I know you're seeing Gloria."

He stared at her in amazement. "*Gloria!*"

Her mouth trembled for just a second; then she turned away. "You haven't touched me in weeks— I'm not stupid. I know when something's wrong! I want to know what I did that made you feel this way toward me!"

He felt his temper starting to come alive again, but he tried to control it. "I told you. There's a level of success I want to reach before—"

"Before *what!* Before you'll forgive me for being who I am? Why should my *father* have anything to do with us? I love you, Morgan. I hate to see you dragging in the door so tired you can't even—"

"If you love me, then why haven't you told your father about us?" He hadn't meant to ask her, but now he was glad it was out in the open.

He watched her face as a blush ran up her neck, into her cheeks.

"Hmm?" Not wanting to see any more, he stalked into the bedroom.

He was changing his clothes when she walked in.

"He would never understand."

"I'll bet he wouldn't—at least we agree on that."

"Morgan, I've told you my father is very old-fashioned! It's not that I'm ashamed of you! If we got married, then—"

"No."

"You said you wanted to marry me. We talked about it that one time—"

"That was before I knew. Now things are different."

"Why? I still love you. We could go to the States. Maybe Dad could help—"

"*No!*" He tucked his shirt into dress slacks and reached for his jacket.

"Where are you going this time?" she asked dully.

"To a party. There's this man I met who—"

"I won't be here when you get back."

"Delia, don't say things you don't mean."

"I mean it."

"We'll talk when I get back—"

"I won't be here! I hate the way we are with each other! Ever since you found out about my father, you've been punishing me for it! I didn't tell people because I wanted to make friends of my *own*, not people who wanted to meet me because of my family."

"Did you think that of me?" The air in the small bedroom seemed suddenly heavy.

"No! I knew you liked me for myself!"

"Delia, I have to do this. I don't ever want anyone to say I rode to the top on your apron strings. This meeting is very important. If I get money from the film, we can get married, and *then* I'll meet your father. But I can't—"

"Daddy doesn't judge people like that! He'd like you *now*, Morgan! He wouldn't care what kind of money you had. He'd like you for the person you are. He's a good guy. He wouldn't—"

"I won't do it any other way. I'll be back by midnight."

"Can I come with you?" She was beginning to cry, and it was twisting his insides.

"No, not this time. But when I come back—"

"Is Gloria going to be there?"

"You know she is. He wants her to be in the film—"

"I'm coming with you!"

"No!"

He'd left her then and run down the stairs, out into the bitter December evening. The meeting had been providential; everything had been perfect. On the way home he stopped for a bottle of champagne and bought a single red rose from the all-night stand. He'd run up the stairs two at a time. It was only ten after midnight.

He'd come into the flat bursting with energy, feeling happier than he had in ages.

But she wasn't there.

He stayed inside for three days, waiting for her to come back, though deep inside a part of him knew she'd left him forever. She'd taken all her clothes but only a few of the books they'd bought together. The little stuffed dog was still on the bed.

On the fourth day he began to pack everything up. He moved the boxes into storage and gave notice to the landlady downstairs. Before the week was up, he was flying to Ireland to make the film.

Success wasn't at all like he thought it would be.

"MORGAN, wake up!"

He shot up in bed, his body covered with sweat. He reached for her and drew her against him. *She's still here.*

"You're shaking!" She drew him down against her, cradling him in her arms as if he were a small child. He buried his face against her shoulder, ashamed she should see him this way.

She stroked his hair for a long time, until the trembling stopped. He eased away from her and turned over. "I'm sorry."

"What's wrong?" She touched his shoulder.

"A dream—it's stupid. Nothing."

"It had to be something for you to be crying out like that." She tugged at his shoulder with the gentlest pressure, and he rolled over so that he faced her.

"It was nothing."

"Tell me, Morgan."

When he didn't say anything, she whispered, "Let me be strong for you."

"I feel like such a . . . fool."

"No. You can tell me anything, Morgan."

It was so hard. He felt as if his chest were breaking apart beneath the strength of his emotions. "Tell me what's going to happen after filming is finished."

She was quiet for a long time, and he closed his eyes.

"You mean us?" she whispered.

"Yes."

He felt her put her arms around his neck and move her body against his. "I don't know. I just know I want us to be together," she said softly.

"Are you sure?"

"Yes."

"I can't take it a second time."

"Was that it? Was that what you were dreaming about?"

He hesitated for a second, then nodded.

She kissed his cheek, then his lips. "I'll never leave you. I couldn't if I wanted to. I love you so much, Morgan, it's like you're a part of me."

He sighed, then hugged her tightly. The words came out slowly as he searched for them. "You're the only good thing that's ever happened to me. I want you to know that."

She answered him with a kiss, and he responded, wanting to be as close to her as possible. Wanting to know that when he woke in the morning she would still be beside him.

BUT HE COULDN'T SLEEP that night, so he left the warmth of their bed and silently walked toward the barn. Outside, the evening was quiet and cool. Morgan had never known silence this intense. It surrounded the night, causing the few sounds to travel great distances. He breathed in the pure, pine-scented air and thought of Delia, back in his bed. But she didn't trust him with whatever was bothering her.

The barn was clearly visible in the bright moonlight. There was an outside light on the side of the building, and he leaned on the rail farthest away, in the darkness.

When would Delia trust him enough to tell him what was on her mind? They were close in so many ways—their talks, their lovemaking, the newfound relaxation and trust when they worked together.

Yet there was still one more bridge to be crossed. There was an important part of her she kept separate from him. And the only thing he knew was that he wanted to share her problems as well as her happiness.

One of the horses in the barn snorted, then kicked his box stall. Morgan smiled grimly. He understood the feeling. He'd tried to be patient with Delia, given her countless opportunities to open up to him, to talk about what was troubling her. And why did it always seem to come back to the picture? She was obsessed with it. He watched her as she worked, careful not to let her see he was observing her. Her blue eyes were always troubled, the frown lines on her forehead always there. He'd had moments when he'd wanted to stop everything and give her a reassuring embrace. Not patronizing, simply asking her to lay down what was troubling her.

Over and over he thought of the various things it might be. Directing the film was a big step in her career. Did she think she wasn't up to it? She brought something special to the film that all the actors had sensed and responded to. A caring, a perspective that was totally devoid of personal ego. If he was honest with himself,

Morgan had to admit she was one of the best directors he'd ever worked with.

Her father? But he'd asked her, and Delia had said he was simply not as strong as he'd once been. And Delia wasn't the sort of person to worry about something without reason.

Their relationship? He frowned, then looked up at the sky, at the thousands of stars in the clear night. It was fine for both of them to talk about how they were going to continue their relationship, but perhaps she was worried about what was really going to happen. If either of their past performances was anything to go by, they both had reason to be worried.

That had to be the problem. It had been difficult at first for both of them. But she had made the first step, had sent the script over for him to read, had invited him to her father's party. She had been the first to put her heart on the line.

He had responded by being as bitter as possible, by throwing barbs in her face and keeping her in constant turmoil both in Los Angeles and on the ranch, by threatening to quit. He wasn't proud of anything he had done, and he didn't believe that his simple apology or Delia's acceptance absolved him of the burden of having behaved like a first-class fool. And it had only been because he'd been scared.

Aren't you scared now, by refusing to make a commitment? He lowered his head into his hands and listened to the sounds of the night—the gentle rustling of the wind, the soft nickers of the horses. The moon shone so brightly it cast a silver glow over the mountains in the distance. He thought of Delia, warm and soft in his bed, and was tempted to stop thinking and go back and make love to her. Yet he had to face what his real feelings were.

You still don't think you're good enough for her. Admit it. When he raised his head and looked blindly into the distance, he knew with a feeling of deep certainty that it was true. Though he had amassed a fortune, worked like someone possessed, built a career that was astounding in its breadth and scope, he still felt he never quite measured up. Delia was an unattainable goal. He'd known it from the first moment he'd seen her.

No one can love her the way I do. He fought with his conscience, wanting more than anything to believe it was possible for them to have a life together.

But are you the best person for her? For what she needs in a man? He remembered the feelings of inadequacy that had flooded him when they'd talked about their childhoods. Delia had told him stories of French finishing schools, skiing trips to Gstaad, vacations on the Riviera. She'd been in the news from the time she was born, had been on a movie set before she knew how to walk.

He'd been fighting to stay alive.

He'd told her a few memories. He'd told her about the first time he'd made love to a girl. But he hadn't told her it had been one of the first times since his mother's death he'd been touched gently.

There was so much he didn't even know about himself. He knew very little about his mother and father. Who had they been? Why hadn't his mother had any family to help her after his father had died?

Why hadn't anyone wanted him?

And she was the daughter of the king of Hollywood, the queen of French cinema. She had chosen him as her first lover. He had let her down even then. He should have stopped, should never have made love to her when he found out she was a virgin. Even then his passion had outweighed his common sense.

He had known from the first moment he'd seen her that they were totally unsuited to each other.

He walked around the corral slowly, trying to decide what he was going to do. By the fifth time around and back, he'd decided.

Let her make the decision. Ask her to get married. You make the commitment, and have the guts to see if she'll have you.

Being here in Wyoming with Delia and her family had brought him to this decision. He had listened with concealed fascination when she'd told him about the summers she'd spent on the ranch. Of course, at that time he hadn't known her father was an actor. But still, he'd envied her the closeness of her family, imagined how they must seem. Tom, his face wrinkled from squinting in the sun, riding in the wind and rain and cold. James, a great bear of a man, an odd combination of gruffness and charm. And Mary, endlessly caring and patient, always looking after everyone. They were good people, and he could only hope some of that goodness had rubbed off on him. It made him understand how Delia had turned out the way she had. Including her mother, Danielle, whom he had met once in Paris on their way to Italy, Delia had been shaped by a remarkable array of people.

When he walked silently back into his bedroom, Delia was still asleep. He undressed slowly, then got into bed beside her. But he didn't touch her. He simply looked at her for a long time before he finally fell asleep.

Chapter Nine

Delia rinsed the last of the soapsuds from the large pot Mary had made chili in, then set it in the dish drain to dry. She wiped her hands on a towel, then began to wipe down the kitchen counters with a sponge.

She welcomed the mindless routine of the chore, wanted to blank out the future.

James had finished the picture. But giving out all that energy had cost him. Mary was by his side constantly, except when Tom took over for brief stretches. Delia rushed to his side at the end of each shooting day and spent weekends with him.

I should have never attempted it. Yet the second the thought came to her, she dismissed it. Even if she'd thrown money away, it had been justified on a human level. Her father had been happy again, in his element, for one brief shining hour.

The kitchen door opened, and she turned to see Morgan come in. The cool evening air gave his face color, and his hands were buried deep in the pockets of his jacket. He unbuttoned his jacket but kept it on.

"Working hard?" His voice was gentle, his dark eyes concerned.

"I just finished. Why weren't you at dinner?"

"I had an errand to do in town, so I asked Mary if I could take the station wagon in." He seemed nervous, and this was so unlike Morgan that Delia frowned slightly.

"Would you like some coffee and apple pie?"

"Only if you sit with me."

She cut him a piece of Mary's pie and poured him a cup of coffee, cleaning up after herself as she did.

"This is very good," Morgan commented after he took a sip of coffee, then reached for his fork.

"Did you eat anything tonight?"

"I grabbed a hamburger in town." He took another sip. "Mary makes good coffee."

"Mary makes good everything. There have been so many times I've wished I was as talented as she was."

He set down his fork and put a hand over hers. "You have other talents, so many that you're unaware of."

Morgan continued to hold her hand, making no effort to eat his pie or drink his coffee.

"I'm going in to see James. Would you like to come with me?" Delia asked, aware that he wanted to be with her.

"Take a walk with me first." His eyes were burning with a peculiar intensity. There was something very different about this moment.

They stepped outside, Morgan still in his

jacket, Delia in a warm red pullover, jeans and boots. Morgan took her arm, and they started to walk away from the house, in the direction of the barn. They walked until they were on the far side of the fence; then Morgan stopped.

He cupped her face in his hands and spoke softly. "I want you to think about this before you answer."

She looked up at him, puzzled. What was he talking about?

"Delia—"

For just an instant his face looked more vulnerable than she'd ever seen it.

"I love you very much. Will you marry me?"

Of all the things she'd thought he was going to ask her, this was the very last. She stared at him for a long moment, then started to smile. Without a second's hesitation, she nodded her head.

"Yes." The last of their problems could be worked out with love.

He stepped closer so that their bodies were touching and lowered his head to kiss her. It was the sweetest of kisses, almost shy. He surprised her once again. Gone was the arrogant, forceful Morgan she was used to, and in his place was a vulnerable man in love.

"I'm glad you said yes." He laughed shakily. "I didn't have anything planned if you'd said no."

"How could you even think I'd refuse you!"

He simply kissed her again, and she could feel his heart pounding rapidly through his open jacket.

When she was able to think coherently again,

she grasped his sleeve and said, "Let's tell James and Mary."

He nodded his head slowly, and they headed back in the direction of the ranch house.

James was sitting by the fire, Mary at his side knitting a sweater.

"Dad?" Delia called softly.

He opened his eyes and smiled at her, a tired expression on his face.

"Dad." She sat down next to him on the leather hassock. "Morgan and I are going to get married."

He looked as if he hadn't heard her for a moment; then his face creased into a smile, and he closed his eyes. When he opened them again, they were suspiciously bright.

"I give you both my blessings." He included Morgan in the loving look he gave Delia. "I was hoping this would happen." Delia watched as he sat up in his chair, and energy seemed to fill his body. "Mary, we need champagne, and where's Tom? This calls for a toast." Extending his hand, he clasped Morgan's firmly. "Welcome to the family, son."

Morgan slowly sat down next to Delia on the hassock. She felt him by her, and it seemed as if tension were leaving his body. She took his hand and gave it a squeeze. Living totally for the moment, Delia basked in the warmth of the room, in a happiness that was palpable.

Once the champagne had been poured, James raised his fluted glass, and a hush fell over the room.

"To Morgan and Delia. May your marriage be filled with warmth and laughter, love and happiness. May you be a constant source of joy and strength to each other. May you always take care of each other." His dark blue eyes were bright. "Delia, I love you very much. Morgan, there isn't another man in the country I would rather my daughter marry. Thank you for the good news." And with that he lifted his glass to his lips. Everyone did the same, and soon the room was bubbling with conversation.

Morgan touched her arm. "I didn't give you your ring yet," he said softly.

"You bought a ring?" she asked, her eyes shining with pleasure. "When did you do that?"

"This afternoon." He reached into the pocket of his jacket and took out a small velvet box and handed it to her.

Delia opened it slowly, then caught her breath. An exquisitely cut, sparkling diamond. It winked up at her, giving off fiery lights.

"Oh." It was all she could think of to say.

He took the ring out of the box and slid it on her finger. A perfect fit.

"How did you know my size?"

"Mary. I asked her this morning."

When Delia looked up at her stepmother, she saw tears running down her face. "Thank you, Delia. This means so much to both of us. Morgan, you have no idea how happy I am."

Delia watched as Morgan kissed Mary softly on her cheek, then shook hands with Tom. Her father, sitting back in his chair, fairly glowed with contentment.

They stayed for close to an hour; then Mary signaled Delia with her eyes that James was tiring.

"We're going to leave you to your fire," Delia announced, taking Morgan's hand and standing up. "I'll see you all in the morning."

She kissed Mary and Tom good-night, then knelt down by her father. "I'll see you tomorrow," she said softly, then kissed his cheek.

"Good night, my princess." Delia felt her throat tighten. He hadn't used her pet name in years. "I love you."

She squeezed his hand. "Always, Daddy."

"Morgan," her father said softly.

"Yes, sir." Morgan knelt so his face was level with James's.

"Take good care of her for me."

"I will."

"I'm entrusting her to you. I want you to know you have someone very special in Delia."

"I know, James. I love her very much, and I'll try to always do what's right for her."

"Make her happy. Don't let her brood too much. And never let a day go by without telling her how much she means to you."

"Dad!" Delia was embarrassed.

"I will."

Back in Morgan's bedroom, Delia felt restless and uneasy. James had looked so tired, but so happy, when they'd told him. He had been right all along when he'd said she and Morgan were well suited.

"What are you thinking about?"

She took off her boots and sweater, then lay down on the bed. "How happy he was. How much he wanted us to get married."

"He did?" Morgan seemed pleased.

"He told me so right after I first came out here. He said you and I were perfectly suited for one another, that we would never be bored."

"He was right."

She didn't want to think about her father. She wanted to forget everything, if only for an instant.

"Morgan?" She opened her eyes.

"Hmm?" He was watching her, as if he were trying to see inside her head.

"Make love to me. Please."

He came to her then, and she forgot everything but the fire that had always existed between them.

DELIA DIDN'T SLEEP well that night, and she was awake by five. Knowing she wouldn't be able to fall back asleep, she got up out of bed and began to dress.

"Where are you going?" Morgan asked sleepily.

"Out to see the sunrise."

"Want some company?"

She felt selfish then, always buried in her private thoughts. This man was as good as her husband. She nodded her head. "I'd like it a lot."

Once outside, they walked over to the corral and faced the mountains. The sky was dark lavender, but the palest tinge of sunlight was visible at the edge of the horizon.

"Beautiful," Morgan murmured.

Delia tucked her hand in his arm and leaned against him. In the face of such stark beauty, she felt desolate. What was the matter with her? The sunrise had never failed to soothe her before.

She heard some noise from the barn; then Falstaff came galloping into the corral, his large hooves thundering against the packed earth. He neighed, and the noise came out an angry squeal.

Tom joined them at the rail. "I don't know what's gotten into him. He was restless all night. I had to come down to his stall in the middle of the night. He was banging his hooves against it."

Falstaff came up to the rail and snorted. Delia reached over and began to pat the silken head. "It's okay, boy. It's okay." She pitched her voice low, and the singsong quality seemed to quiet the animal.

"He's the steadiest horse we've got. He just has to be ridden more often." Tom seemed worried.

The sun was rising in the sky, washing the pale morning light with tinted hues of pink and gold.

"There's nothing like this anywhere else in the world," Delia said softly as Morgan's arm tightened around her.

They watched the sunrise silently. Falstaff trotted to the far end of the corral and began to buck, his massive hooves kicking against the fence. The clanging, harsh sound carried in the still morning air.

"Hey, now!" Tom leaped into the corral and began to run toward the horse.

"I don't know what's wrong with him," she said to Morgan. "He's usually the sweetest boy—"

"*Delia!*" Mary stood on the kitchen steps. Even from a distance Delia could see that her face was contorted with pain.

No.

Her heart began to pound at a sickeningly fast pace, and she started to walk, then run, toward her stepmother.

MORGAN STOOD FROZEN at the fence as the final piece of the puzzle and realization came crashing down around him.

He was dying. My God. She made the film because he was dying.

Tom was at the fence moments after Delia left. Tears were running down his face, and he made no attempt to disguise his grief.

"God be with you, James Wilde," he said softly.

"I'm entrusting her to you." James's words came back to Morgan with new meaning. They were not simply the words of a pleased father-in-law; he had asked Morgan to take care of his daughter for all time.

"Make her happy." All he could think of was the hell he had put her through, the things he had accused her of. Greed. Nepotism. Selfishness.

And she hadn't told him.

He started toward the kitchen door, wanting to be with her at this time, then stopped. Who was he to barge into a family's private grief when all he had done from the start was make Delia's filming experience miserable? Why should he suddenly have the right to atone for what he had done?

Emotions warred within him as he struggled to do what he thought was best for Delia.

You love her. You should be with her. She needs you.

You put her through hell. You almost walked out. He didn't know if he could ever forgive himself.

Go to her. He took a few steps toward the kitchen door, then stopped.

He didn't know what to do.

Turning abruptly, he started toward the guest house, his shoulders tightly hunched.

DELIA'S HANDS SHOOK as she opened the door to her father's bedroom. Everything was so still. Mary was behind her, clutching her hand.

"I woke up just a few minutes ago. He always kicked the covers off on his side of the bed, but they were still around him. I couldn't hear him breathing, so I touched his feet with mine, and they were cold—" She broke off as they entered the room.

The minute Delia saw her father, she knew he had died in his sleep. Completely numb, she walked slowly to the side of the bed, then put her fingers on his forehead. He was so very still.

She couldn't feel anything except emptiness. Turning toward Mary, she took the older woman in her arms and held her tightly. She didn't want to remember her father that way. She had to get Mary out of the bedroom.

"He's gone, Mary." They were the hardest words she'd ever said in her life.

"But he can't be! He was so happy last night, Delia. He was talking to me about you and Morgan and how happy he was. I made him a cup of tea; then I rubbed his feet and tucked him into bed—"

Morgan. Tom. Where are you? "Sit down, Mary, and let me—"

"He looked so good! It must be his heart! Maybe his heart—"

"Come with me, Mary." She put her arm around her stepmother's shoulders and led her into the kitchen. Sitting her down at the table, she held her hands tightly. Why didn't someone come?

"Mary." Delia almost started to cry when she heard Tom's voice, gentle but firm. "Let me make you some tea."

Mary passed a hand weakly over her eyes. "He always kicked the covers off on his side of the bed—"

Delia couldn't bear hearing it again. Walking quickly into the living room, she dialed the operator.

Her voice shook when she started to talk. "I don't know who I'm supposed to call, but there's been a death in my family—"

The woman was wonderful, talking to her until she had an accurate address, making sure Delia wasn't alone. When she finally hung the phone up, Delia walked woodenly into the kitchen. The sun was shining brightly over Mary and Tom, and there was a steaming mug of tea in Mary's hands.

She could hear Tom talking to Mary as if she were one of the horses he trained. "Drink that, now; that's good. There's honey in it; it's good for you."

Delia couldn't stand to be in the house a moment longer. She ran out the door and kept running, passing the corral and barn, until she reached the guest house. Morgan. She had to see him.

He was just coming out the door, and she ran into his chest. Delia felt his arms come around her in a crushing embrace. She held on to him tightly. He was the only strong and stable thing in her world. Everything else had been rocked off its foundation.

She couldn't cry. She felt as if she were out of her body, numb, as if it were happening to someone else. Delia pressed her cheek against Morgan's shirtfront, and she felt his hand come up and smooth her hair.

He didn't say anything, just walked with her slowly to the main house, then sat with her on the kitchen steps, facing the long driveway.

It was the cruelest of nightmares. The sun was shining brightly, the wind gentle on her face. Somehow Delia had expected the sky to boil with black clouds or the wind to whistle violently down from the mountains. But the weather was absolutely beautiful.

She held on to Morgan's hand tightly and felt absolutely nothing as she sat on the kitchen steps and watched the silent ambulance make its way up the winding country road.

Chapter Ten

The rest of the day had an air of unreality. Once the ambulance came and took James away, Delia wandered around the ranch house, wondering how everything could still look the same. The sun was high in the sky, the weather serene. Several quarter horses still grazed out in the paddock, and Hades pranced restlessly in the corral.

Morgan stayed by her side constantly. While Tom comforted Mary, Delia was conscious of Morgan watching over her. He looked awful; his face was pale, his eyes dark with pain. Yet he answered phone calls, talked to neighbors as they dropped by with casseroles, salads, loaves of homemade bread, all sorts of foodstuffs. As she watched the food pile up on the kitchen table, Delia felt detached from it all, as if she were acting a part in a play. She never wanted to eat again, so why were people bringing food?

Yet the people in the valley were a great comfort to Mary. Except for summers and some holidays, Delia hadn't spent her adult life at the ranch. But Mary and James had had a life here. As people kept coming in the door, offering help in any way they could, Delia slowly realized how many friends James and Mary had, how much they were loved.

Early that evening, as the sun began to set over the mountains, Delia pushed open the kitchen door and walked out to the corral. She had to get away—from all the people, the smell of food, the endless condolences. There was something within her that needed the wide open space the ranch provided. Somehow she felt closer to her father when she walked the land.

Falstaff was out behind the barn, in one of the paddocks. When the massive quarter horse saw her, his large ears perked up slightly, and he began to walk slowly toward the rail.

Delia scratched behind his ears gently, absently. The thought of her father never riding his favorite horse brought quick stinging tears to her eyes, but she pushed them back. She couldn't cry for James. Not yet.

She heard quiet footsteps behind her but didn't need to turn. Morgan. He came up beside her at the rail but didn't touch her. She watched as he ran a hand over Falstaff's neck, then gently touched the horse's forelock.

"Are you coming in for dinner?" he asked quietly.

She concentrated on patting Falstaff. "No. I'll eat something later."

"Delia, tell me what you need. Tell me how to help you."

Her restless hand stilled, but only for a moment. "I've been thinking, Morgan." She had to force herself to say the next words. Delia knew if she let herself go emotionally, even the tiniest little bit, she wouldn't get back up for a long time. She wanted to lock herself in her bedroom and cry for days, deny that anything had changed. But right now she couldn't afford the luxury of tears. She had work she had to finish. And a deadline.

She cleared her throat. "There is something you can help me with."

"Anything."

"I want to finish the film."

He was silent for a minute, but when he spoke, his voice was quiet. "Do you have enough footage of your father?"

She nodded. "I knew we wouldn't have much time once we got here. All I wanted to film at the ranch was exteriors, and we just made it."

"So the principle work to be finished is with Belinda and me."

"Yes."

He placed a reassuring hand on her arm and squeezed gently. "Then we'll do it. Whatever it takes, we'll finish the film."

She put her hand over his and touched the warmth of his skin. "Thank you, Morgan."

THAT NIGHT, in Delia's bedroom, Morgan couldn't sleep. The ranch house was finally quiet for the night. Even King seemed to have accepted his master's death. The shepherd had just about broken Morgan's heart, waiting silently by the dinner table, then the fire. Every time the door had opened, King's muzzle had lifted, his large liquid eyes expectant. But by the end of the day he seemed to understand James wasn't coming back and had slowly trotted down the hall and stationed himself at Mary's bedroom door.

Morgan lay apart from Delia, watching her sleep. She slept like one exhausted, breathing deeply and not moving. Her face was turned into the pillow, the covers bunched protectively around her shoulders.

He hadn't been sure what his place was tonight by the fire. He had sat up with Delia after Mary retired, had assumed he'd go back to the guest house, giving Delia some time alone, though that was the last thing he wanted. He didn't want to make love; he simply wanted to be with her, to protect her.

She'd answered his question when she'd stood up and taken his hand, then walked down the hall to her bedroom. She'd undressed quietly, then slid underneath the covers into his arms. He'd held her until she fell asleep.

He stared up at the ceiling, willing sleep to come and silence the thoughts whirling through his mind. Why hadn't she cried? Mary finally had, when she'd walked out to call Tom in for dinner and seen Falstaff in the corral. It didn't seem right, she'd said later, to see the horse without James.

But Delia remained impassive. He'd watched her as she'd pushed her food around her plate, then while she'd sat by the fire, her thoughts a million miles away. On the film.

He wondered if he'd been wise to agree to help her. Morgan sighed, then stretched his arms and folded them behind his head. But it seemed they were so close to finishing. And it meant so much to her. It would only be a matter of a few weeks. Then—

Then he hoped she would agree to marry him. Not right away. But at least they could be together. He knew he would stay on at the ranch, if that was what she or Mary needed.

He studied her face again, and convinced she was deeply asleep, he slid out of bed and turned on the small television set by the bed, keeping the volume low. He flipped through the channels until he found a late-night news show, then settled back to watch.

Anything to take his mind off the day.

What he hadn't counted on was James's death being an event of national importance. Before he could switch the dial, there was a clip of James in one of his earliest films. It was a particularly moving scene, and Morgan watched, unable to tear his eyes away.

What followed was a short documentary on James's life and career. How he'd broken into the business. His first successful films. His marriage to Danielle. Delia. Morgan watched, fascinated, as picture after picture filled the small screen. Danielle and James, on their wedding day. James holding Delia as a baby, her chubby fingers wrapped tightly around his finger. Delia on a pony, her cowboy hat down on her shoulders, her hair flying out behind her. A picture of James, Mary and Delia, with a much younger King panting at their feet.

He couldn't get up and change the dial. Delia had never talked to him about so much of her life—but when had he let her? After he'd found out she was James Wilde's daughter, he'd effectively silenced any communication they might have had. Morgan watched as a life unfolded on screen.

And he began to understand. Sometime during filming, while living and working at the ranch, he'd finally let go of his past. Perhaps it had been the way James and Mary had welcomed him, made him feel like part of a family. Perhaps it had been when he and Delia had become lovers again. Or maybe it was simply the vast Wyoming skies, the endless expanse of mountains, that put everything into perspective and made him realize nothing could be that bad when he had people to love and a fire to sit by.

The change had happened so slowly, so gently, that he hadn't even noticed. As he watched the news report come to an end, Morgan got up off the bed and turned off the set. The room was dark again as he stretched out on his side of the bed, careful not to jostle Delia.

How had he ever thought it could have been easy, being James Wilde's daughter? He remembered the time she'd told him she hadn't wanted anyone to know who she was, had wanted people to like her for herself. Would he have even gone near her if he'd known?

And he thought of his own bitterness, the feelings of inadequacy that had chased him all his life. That had probably been the prime motivation for his becoming an actor. To force people into looking at him, paying attention—realizing he was worth something, after all.

He'd been scared to ask her to marry him, but he wasn't scared anymore. Sliding down under the covers, Morgan eased across the mattress until he was close to Delia.

She was turned toward him, and he studied her delicate features, seeing the exhaustion etched on her face. Carefully, so as not to wake her, he smoothed the hair off her forehead, then kissed it gently.

No one can love you the way I do. His thoughts filled his heart as he watched her, and her face was the last thing he saw before he closed his eyes and finally slept.

THE NEXT TWO WEEKS seemed to fly by, and Morgan remembered them as a time of hard work and feverish intensity. He watched Delia, and it seemed to him the film consumed her. She barely took time to eat or sleep, she was so intent on making sure everything was perfect.

His and Belinda's final scenes caught fire, the emotions blazing between their characters honest and true. There was no safety net for the risks they took as actors. It was James's death,

Morgan was certain, that gave their performances such a fine edge. The older actor had given them all a chance to see their own mortality.

Evenings were spent quietly in front of the fire after Delia studied the dailies, and he watched as she looked after Mary. He was amazed by this, because Delia certainly didn't have any strength to spare. Yet she was always available for her stepmother, making her a cup of tea, running into town to get her some yarn for her latest afghan.

And Delia was good to the crew. She didn't seem to expect them to share her intensity over the project. She still gave them Sundays off and managed to finish filming most days at a reasonable hour. No one could accuse her of being a slave driver.

She reserved that privilege for herself.

He never saw her without a piece of the script in her hands, without a worried frown on her face. Part of each evening was spent on the phone to Los Angeles, talking to the editors she'd lined up for the final cut, conferring with her godfather, Bob Rosenthal. There never seemed to be a moment when she let the film go. Even in sleep he could see the tension in her face.

They didn't make love, and he understood. All her energy was going toward the film. And Morgan didn't resent it. He understood there was a deadline to be met, a very personal deadline in Delia's own mind.

He could wait.

What he couldn't deal with was the guilt that overcame him when he thought about how he'd held up production. He hadn't realized James was so ill, but still Morgan chastised himself. His thoughts became a silent litany. If only, if only . . .

So he faced the final scene in the picture, when he confronted Mary Anne with how he felt about her, with the feeling that he had to give Delia something. He wanted to make up for what he'd put her through during the beginning of filming.

He didn't talk with Delia the morning of their final day of shooting. He got up early, had a quick cup of coffee with Mary and walked out to where the scene took place. And he began to build his energy, get into character, visualize the scene as he wanted it to go.

He ran lines briefly with Belinda before they walked in front of the cameras. And there was Delia, the same tense expression on her face, her eyes moving restlessly, taking in everything. Checking.

Wanting to wipe that harried look off her face, he walked to her side and took her elbow in his hand.

"Are you feeling okay?" he asked.

She nodded quickly. Too quickly. "Ready to go?"

"Whenever you are." He cupped her face in both his hands, not caring who saw them or what they thought. "Delia, I'm doing this for you."

He kissed her swiftly, then stepped back and

turned around. Without looking back, he headed toward Belinda.

There were no false starts this time. The cameras rolled, Delia called "action," and he slipped effortlessly into the character.

If he had one failing as an actor, it was that sometimes he fell back on technique instead of giving over to emotion. And his technique was so good, he could get away with it and still come out looking terrific.

Not this time. There was no safe place for Morgan to retreat as he began the scene. He and Belinda had rehearsed it just enough so they were comfortable with each other but not enough so that the spontaneity was lost. He was confident she would follow him wherever he led her.

It was the final scene, where Mary Anne had to decide whether she wanted to go with him or not. And Morgan's character had to convince her.

He reached inside himself for the deepest emotions and imbued the scene with a full range of feelings. Anger and frustration, certainly. But fear and vulnerability, as well. He used his own feelings, his fears over whether he and Delia would ever find a place in time to call their own.

Raw and hurting, his insides twisting with the intensity of his emotions, he walked woodenly toward his horse. The scene was almost over, and Mary Anne had chosen to stay.

He swung himself up into the saddle, grasped the reins and pulled gently, making the pinto gelding back up slowly, away from the rail.

Then he felt hands on his stirruped foot. They moved higher, up his leg, until Belinda was clasping his hand.

He looked down at her. She was staring up at him, defiant and vulnerable at the same time. Her emotions were held in check; her fingers trembled as they touched his.

"Don't go." It was the most poignant of whispers.

He dismounted slowly, took her into his arms and crushed her to him. His body trembled as he held her, and she started to cry. It was all there—all the emotion, the intensity, the love.

He held her until he heard Delia's voice say softly, "That's it."

Morgan released Belinda and stepped back, giving her upper arms a friendly squeeze. "You were really cooking."

She ran her fingers over her cheeks and smiled up at him through her tears. "Thanks, Morgan."

Releasing her completely, he looked over at Delia. Her eyes were luminous, filled with tears. Slowly, she smiled, then nodded her head.

All the air seemed to leave his lungs at the same time, and his legs trembled slightly. He'd done it. Given her, in the space of one scene, the best work of his career. He felt his feelings of guilt finally slip away.

The crew was quietly packing away its equipment as Morgan stepped carefully around people until he stood next to Delia.

"You did it," he said softly.

She stared up at him, her mouth soft and vulnerable, her eyes clouded. Then, without saying a word, she looped her arms around his waist and pressed herself against him, her cheek against his leather vest.

His hands came up as if they had a will of their own, one to the small of her back, the other to cradle her head and stroke her hair. He felt a deep shudder course through her body and pressed his lips against her hair.

Let it out. You can cry now; it's finished.

But she simply held on tighter, pressed her face against his chest and stood perfectly still.

THAT EVENING, at dinner, Mary made fried chicken to celebrate.

Morgan sat back in his chair. He'd never really appreciated Mary's strength until now. She was quietly going on with her life. Not even three weeks after James's death, she was managing the ranch, seeing to everyone else. She'd arranged for several of James's scripts, complete with his notes, to be shipped to a New York film museum. At the same time, she was also going through family photographs and preparing to meet a reporter—a close personal friend—to talk about James.

She'd let him go.

He glanced over at Delia and watched her push pieces of chicken around her plate. She'd barely touched her food. He could understand. She was still wound up over finishing the film.

When Mary began to clear the table, Delia gave up her plate.

"I have apple pie and cinnamon ice cream for dessert," Mary announced. "Your favorite, Morgan."

He loved her for her kindness. "I think I can manage a slice." He grinned.

"Tom?" Mary asked.

He winked at her. "Sure, you couldn't chase me away from the table, knowing your pie's on the way."

"Delia?"

"I'll have mine later, Mary." She pushed her chair away from the table, her brow wrinkled in thought. "I've got to give Bob a call before it gets too late. I'll be back in a little bit."

Morgan watched her leave, the set of her back rigid and straight as she headed toward her bedroom. He continued to stare after her until Mary set his pie down in front of him. When he picked up his fork, he found he had no appetite.

The film was far from over.

THE MORNING THEY LEFT for Los Angeles, Morgan got up early and showered, then headed out toward the barn. He stopped when he reached the corral, leaned on the fence and watched as Hades circled the enclosure restlessly.

There was something soothing about watching the animal move, watching sleek muscles ripple underneath the black satin coat. It was almost hypnotizing, lulling his mind into relaxation.

Tom had worked miracles in the time he'd trained the Arabian. The animal was beginning to trust again. Quite an achievement, even for Tom.

When he heard Mary's voice, he started, then quickly turned around.

"I didn't mean to startle you, Morgan." She walked up and joined him at the rail.

He ran his fingers through his hair, massaging his temples as he did so. "I'm just tired. It makes me jumpy."

She was silent for a moment as they both watched the Arabian.

"I want to wait a while before the funeral," Mary said quietly. "James asked me to scatter his ashes at the foot of the mountains." Her expression was determined as she gazed at the horizon. "I won't have it turned into one of those celebrity circuses, but I would like it very much if you would come back with Delia."

He was oddly touched. But he remained silent, sensing there was more on her mind.

"What will happen when you and Delia go back to Los Angeles?" she asked.

Morgan sighed. "We're into the home stretch. She has to edit the film, then show the final cut to the studio."

"When will it be over for her? When do the responsibilities end?"

"A director's involved with every stage of production. The film will have to be edited, then dubbed. Delia said it could take up to eight weeks, and that's if she's lucky. It's supposed to be a Christmas release, and it has to be to qualify for next year's Academy Awards. She's going to get in just under the wire.''

Mary was silent for a moment, her eyes worried as she watched Hades. ''I don't like the way she looks.''

''I don't, either. I wish she'd eat more. She sleeps, but she still seems tired.'' His hands were balled into fists at his sides. ''I don't mean to hurt you, Mary, but I'm beginning to hate this picture. For what it's doing to Delia.''

''I understand.'' She put her hand on his arm. ''You're going to have to take care of her these next few months. Maybe even until the picture opens.''

''I know.'' He hesitated for a moment, then decided to confide in Mary, knowing he could trust her with his deepest feelings. ''She doesn't seem to be— I don't know quite how to say this. It's as if she's keeping all her feeling locked away. You seem to have mourned James, let him go. I keep sensing Delia hasn't let any of her feelings out.''

Mary smiled, but her eyes remained sad. ''They had a difficult relationship, James and Delia. He wanted to be a good father so desperately, but in the earlier years he barely knew how. And then, as his fame grew, it became harder and harder for Delia to be his daughter.'' She sighed. ''It was hard enough to be married to an American institution, let alone being part of the dynasty. Can you understand any of that, Morgan? If you and Delia ever have children, can you imagine what they might go through?"

"I never gave it much thought before coming here."

Mary kept her eyes on Hades the entire time she spoke, as if by not looking at him, it made it easier to speak. "It's been hard on her. I think that deep inside she's always been scared of not measuring up. That's why the picture is so important. It's something she's done alone. Something she can give to him. The sad thing is, all the time James was worried about not being a good father, Delia went through just as much agony trying to be a good daughter."

He gripped the rail tightly. "Did Delia ever tell you— I mean, did you know we knew each other before?"

"I knew."

He couldn't speak.

She turned to face him, her brown eyes warm and trusting. "She came back to the ranch when she left you. James was on location, so it was just the two of us."

"I never meant to hurt her. I wanted to marry her, take care of her."

"I know you did. I know you loved each other very much."

Morgan looked down at his hands on the rail. "If she had trouble being James's daughter, then I had trouble accepting who she was. I had this crazy idea she might think I wanted to use her. When we started seeing each other, I had no idea who she was. Only that I cared for her."

Mary stayed silent, listening.

His hands tightened on the railing. "That's not totally the truth. If I'm honest...Mary, I didn't see how someone like Delia could care for me. She seemed so...far beyond anything I'd ever known."

She put her hand over his and squeezed.

"I...pushed her away from me before she had a chance to...I couldn't have handled her leaving me. But I wanted so much. I wanted to build a life with her, but first—"

"First you had to be a success."

He wasn't surprised she understood.

"She wanted me to meet James, and I couldn't. Not before I'd had some success. And after she left— Mary, there was nothing left for me, no matter how hard I climbed."

"What scares you now, Morgan?"

He stared out in front of him, not seeing the black Arabian circling the corral. "Sometimes I wonder if we'll ever find a time to simply be together. If we'll marry. Both times I've been with Delia we've been caught up in the middle of something crucial."

"I can understand that feeling."

"And now—I fantasize about taking her away from everything. Somewhere tropical. So I can watch her relax, get some color back in her face, start eating and sleeping again. So we can have time to—" He stopped, not wanting to get too personal with Mary.

She patted his arm. "You'll have that time. You have to have some faith, Morgan. Faith that things will work out." She smiled up at him, her eyes serene. "You love her very much, and that's all that matters. Once the film is over, you'll both find a way."

"I promise you I'll take care of her, Mary."

"I know you will. Now let's get both of you on that plane."

Chapter Eleven

The alarm went off, and classical music filled the large bedroom. Delia poked a hand out from underneath the heavy cotton bedspread and shut it off. Willing sensation into her exhausted body, she sat up, rubbed her eyes, drew her fingers through her tangled hair and stood up.

She swayed slightly, but force of will propelled her into the bathroom and a hot shower.

She heard the door swing open as she was shampooing her hair. Then Morgan's voice called out, "What time do you have to be at the studio?"

"We're meeting at six."

"Do you have time for a quick breakfast?"

She poked her head underneath the stinging spray, careful to keep her mouth out of the water. "Morgan, you know I don't eat this early in the morning."

"I'll make you a protein drink, then." He shut the door before she could say anything else.

As she dried herself off, Delia avoided looking

at herself in the mirror. She knew she looked awful. Letting her hair dry naturally, she pulled on a pair of jeans and a deep purple cotton sweater. She got by with the minimum amount of makeup—just enough so she didn't look too hideous—and slipped on a pair of comfortable canvas shoes. No one cared what you looked like in the editing room. She was simply there to work.

They were two weeks into the final cut of the film, and she estimated she had another week to go. She'd been working practically around the clock with three editors in three separate rooms at the studio. Delia was completely aware that proper editing could make or break a film.

She didn't want to look ahead to more weeks of dubbing, putting in sound effects and music and looping in dialogue. If she thought that far, she'd crawl back into the bedroom and pull the covers over her head.

She met Morgan in the kitchen. It was a large room, with windows overlooking the Pacific. The sun was just beginning to rise behind the hills, tinting the water with pale shades.

Delia watched as Morgan poured the protein shake into two tall glasses, then sat down. She picked up her glass and began to drink her breakfast standing up.

"Delia, sit down. You can spare five minutes, can't you?" There was an edge of irritation to his voice.

She sat, continuing to drink the shake. When

she finished, she set the glass down, then sat back in the chair for just an instant.

"What are you up to today?"

"I have a meeting with my agent. Then I thought I'd meet you for lunch and—"

"I don't know when I'll be able to take a break—"

"I'll bring in sandwiches." Morgan stood up and collected both glasses, walked over to the kitchen sink and rinsed them out. "I'll bring something that can't possibly spoil, then camp out on your doorstep until you can't ignore me." He smiled, and she knew he was trying to soften the sound of his words. "You'll have to take pity on me and have lunch."

She got up out of her chair and walked quickly to his side, throwing her arms around him. Burying her face against his chest, her words were muffled.

"I love you." She tightened her grip around his waist. "Just a few more weeks and it will be finished. If we can hang in until then—"

"It's not me I'm worried about," he interjected.

"Morgan, don't start again! I'm fine!" She glanced quickly at the clock over the stove. "I've got to go."

"I'll see you at lunch, okay?"

"Okay."

Fifteen minutes later she was speeding down Pacific Coast Highway, then turning onto the Santa Monica Freeway going east. As she quickly changed lanes, moving all the way over to the far left, her thoughts turned to Morgan.

They'd moved into his beach house. She hadn't been ready to go back to her father's house and all the memories it contained. Morgan had been her rock during the past two weeks, making sure she ate, taking care of the myriad tasks needed to run a household, cooking dinner, but more often bringing food right to the studio. He nagged her if she didn't sleep enough, answered the phone and screened her calls and was there for her.

I'm not being very good to him right now, she thought with a frown as she pushed her speed slightly higher.

You don't have time, she argued back. As soon as that thought formed, another followed.

You can at least be nicer than you have been. It seemed they were always at odds, but time was tight, and the pace was relentless. And it was only going to get worse as the weeks progressed.

When I'm finished, we'll go someplace—to the edge of the world—and not even have a phone. I'll make it up to him when this is all over and I can relax.

Satisfied with her plan, she concentrated on her driving.

"IT WOULD BE EASIER if I just moved in a cot and slept there," Delia commented that same evening. "Look at all the time I waste driving."

Morgan glanced up from the script he was

reading. "Look at all the pleasure I get sleeping next to you."

She flushed softly and walked over to his chair. As the lamplight behind made her body clearly visible through the cotton nightgown, Morgan's eyes narrowed.

She's losing weight.

When she sat down on the arm of his chair, he pulled her into his lap.

"How much do you weigh, Delia?"

She kissed his cheek and snuggled down into his embrace. "I don't know. I haven't been keeping track." She teased his jawline with a finger, running it delicately over his skin. "Are you complaining?"

He could tell she was making a major effort to spend time with him. "You don't have to do this, Delia."

"Do what?"

"You're exhausted. Why don't you go to sleep."

To his surprise, her eyes filled with tears, and she looked away.

"Delia? Tell me."

Instead of answering him, she put her arms around his neck and hugged him very tightly. He circled her with his arms and held her until he could tell by her even breathing she was asleep. Picking her up, Morgan carried her to the bed and tucked her in. He checked the alarm to make sure it was set, then turned off the lights and pulled back the covers, sliding underneath and settling his body against hers.

He ran his hand over her shoulders in a gentle massaging gesture as he thought. *Another week of editing. Then three more weeks—if she's lucky—to finish up all the dubbing.*

He reached his arm around her waist and moved close to her until they were lying like spoons. She seemed so fragile in his arms, as if a strong gesture from him could break her.

Another month. If I can stand it.

DELIA SAT QUIETLY, listening to Michael Belmont as he explained his musical interpretation of the film.

He was a small man with a neat mustache and quick, nervous movements. But he was brilliant at scoring films, and he'd been a friend of her father's.

Michael had visited the set for a week, had soaked up the atmosphere of the ranch, had watched filming. He was an instinctual worker, and once the foundation of his idea was set, he worked quickly and efficiently.

She tried to concentrate.

"And the way the land around the ranch shaped the man, that's what fascinated me. So I used this piece when James first walks on-screen—"

His head seemed to be getting smaller. Delia blinked, clenched her hands into fists so her nails bit into her palm and concentrated.

Listen to him. It's just for another few minutes.

But Michael seemed to be floating away from her, as if she were outside, watching. His mouth was moving, but no sound was coming out of it.

She blinked again, then realized he was waiting for her to answer him.

"Delia?" He sounded slightly impatient. "How does that sound to you?"

She raked her fingers through her hair, surprised to find she was perspiring. The hair around her temples was damp, and her skin felt as if it weren't hers.

"Beautiful." She stood and locked her knees so they wouldn't tremble. "I think it's going to add so much to the film." Silently, she prayed she'd given the temperamental little man the correct response.

He seemed pleased. "Then I'll see you in a few days. Will you be coming to the scoring?"

She nodded her head. They shook hands; then Michael walked quickly out of her make-shift office.

Delia closed the door after him, then sat back down in her chair behind her desk. Her hands were trembling as she covered her face.

Just a little more time. Once the screening is over, you can go home and sleep for days. Just keep going—you have to finish. You're the only one who can do it.

Her thoughts ran through her head, a silent litany. A prayer. She'd said the words so many times, driving in the car. She'd thought them lying in bed at night, too exhausted to sleep.

Just a little more time.

Where the extra reserve of strength came

from, Delia didn't question. She simply sat quietly in her office, her thoughts going to her father. She visualized him during his final scene with Morgan. He'd been in pain, but he'd given it everything he had.

She glanced at her watch. She had another appointment within the hour.

Steeling herself, she got out of her chair and walked determinedly toward the door.

MORGAN MET HER for dinner. He brought sandwiches from a coffee shop and everything else fattening he could buy. Potato and macaroni salad. Several candy bars. A vanilla milk shake.

He saw her before she saw him.

She was talking with someone in the hall, leaning against the wall, looking up at the man she was with. Morgan recognized Bob Rosenthal's spare frame. He stopped before he reached her, wanting her to finish talking with Bob so they could go somewhere and eat.

When she finished, he waved, and she came over. She walked slowly, and as she approached him, she stumbled. Morgan held out his hand and caught her arm.

"Easy," he said softly.

She wrapped her arms around him and hugged him tightly. It seemed to Morgan she was trying to draw strength from him. He kissed the top of her head and heard her take a deep sigh.

They were in the home stretch. But at such a cost. She felt like nothing in his arms, and he wondered grimly how much weight she'd lost.

Her hair was dull, her coloring bad. She'd been irritable with him on so many evenings, but he'd let it pass, knowing she was tired.

He guided her into an empty office, then set the bag down on top of a desk.

She sat on the edge of the desk and watched him as he unpacked the food. As he set container after container in front of her, he was pleased to see the beginnings of a smile on her tired face.

"What did you do, buy out a restaurant?" she asked.

He handed her the milk shake. "Drink this."

She took a sip, then set it down.

Morgan began to unwrap sandwiches. "There's tuna with avocado, cheese and tomato, roast beef and a corned beef on rye."

"All for me?" She picked up half of the tuna and avocado. "What are you going to eat?"

He smiled. If she was able to joke with him, things couldn't be that bad. "Whatever you leave. And for dessert—" He flourished two candy bars dramatically. "I brought you two Snickers bars."

He watched as she made it through half the tuna sandwich, then drank part of the milk shake. She didn't pick up the second half, and he realized she was waiting for him to eat, too. Determinedly, he picked up half of the roast beef.

"Everything is on schedule. Bob is really pleased." Delia seemed to need to talk about the film's progress, so he listened carefully.

"Did Frank call you about looping?" she asked.

He nodded, his mouth full, wishing she'd continue to eat.

She rubbed her thumb and forefinger against the bridge of her nose. "They found a man for James's voice. I listened the other day. Morgan, it was so strange hearing his voice coming out of someone else's mouth."

"I'll bet it was." He folded up some of the papers. "Are you going to eat the rest of that sandwich?" he asked.

"No, I'm full."

"I'll leave the rest with you in case you get hungry later."

She nodded. "I was just talking with—" She stopped, and Morgan knew she'd forgotten what she was going to say.

It clearly upset her. "When you came down the hall. I was talking to—"

"Bob," he supplied gently.

"Bob. He's really pleased the film is on schedule."

He didn't have the heart to tell her she'd just told him.

"I'm proud of you, Delia," he said softly, but there was a worried edge to his tone. "What time do you want me to pick you up?"

She touched his arm and squeezed it. There was almost no pressure to her touch. "I'm going to be late."

"Call me. I'll keep the phone by the bed."

He threw away their garbage, handed her the

bag, gave her a quick kiss and started out the door.

There were times, when she was so very tired, that he couldn't bear to look at her for a long time.

But now it was only a matter of days.

HE WOKE UP slowly. The bedroom was bathed in pale shades of sunrise. Glancing quickly at the bedside clock, Morgan swore softly.

Quarter to six. She'd been at the studio all night again.

He reached for the bedside phone and called the studio number.

Delia's voice on the other end of the line relieved the sudden fear he'd had for her safety but did nothing for the anger slowly building inside him.

"What the hell are you trying to do, kill yourself?"

There was a moment of silence on the other end of the line. Then Delia said softly, "I'm asking you to help me for three more days, Morgan. The screening is this Friday, and after that it's out of my hands."

He remained silent. He couldn't speak.

She was pleading with him now. "I have to do it, Morgan. I have to make sure it's the best it can be. No one cares the way I do. No one feels the same way—" She began to cry softly, and the sound tore him apart inside. It seemed all Delia did lately was cry.

"Let me help you." He had to do something.

"There's nothing you can do you aren't already doing. You finished your looping, you bring me food, you drive me to the studio—Morgan, three more days and we can go away. I promise you. I wouldn't be working this hard if I thought I was going to hurt myself."

He sighed harshly, his emotions barely in check. Suddenly, they began to spill over. He had to tell her how he felt, how if she hurt herself he wouldn't want to go on. How he couldn't bear to lose her again—

"I worry so much. Delia, it's like this film is eating you alive—"

"I have to go, Morgan. They're calling me." She hung up.

He couldn't believe she'd hung up, even as tired and disoriented as he knew she had to be. He stared at the phone in his hand, listening to the dial tone. The buzzing pushed something inside him that had been teetering on the edge of sanity. How could she do this to herself? To the two of them? Couldn't she see how she was hurting herself? And how much it hurt him to watch her?

Morgan exploded.

"Damn you, Delia!" He threw the phone against the bedroom wall, then stared at the mark it made.

"I'LL PICK YOU and Morgan up on my way to the studio tonight, Delia." Bob looked slightly concerned as he studied her flushed face. "Are you sure everything is all right?"

"Fine. So you'll be at Morgan's around seven?"

"That's perfect."

Delia waved at her godfather brightly before he turned the corner in the hallway, then closed her office door. She leaned against it, then doubled over, her arms crossed.

You did it. It's over.

Her hands were trembling as she pressed them against her cheeks. Fever. It was the only thing that could explain why she felt the way she did. She'd been coughing the last two days, feeling dizzy and weak.

You cannot get sick. You don't have time.

She straightened up, every ounce of her will in the simple gesture. Home. She had to go home and change.

You'll feel better after a shower.

She picked up her sweater and bag and, on shaking legs, began the long walk to the car. Morgan had stopped driving her but had arranged for limousine service.

Sleep in the car on the way home. Then you'll feel better.

Knowing she was lying to herself, Delia quickened her pace.

MORGAN LISTENED to the shower running as he toweled his hair dry in the bedroom.

Only one more night of this lunacy and it will be all over.

He'd grown to hate the film because of what it had done to Delia. The last week had been the worst. The film was right on schedule; it had been finished exactly eight weeks after they flew back from Wyoming.

She seemed to come to life only at the studio, and then it was by sheer effort of will. He'd come to expect her mood swings, from her jittery, wired high to the lethargic, empty low. He'd continued to bring her food but hadn't had the heart to stay around and make sure she ate it.

She's a big girl, he thought, his mood foul. *She can take care of herself.*

The minute he saw her step into their bedroom, he admitted the lie.

As she slowly unwound the thick blue towel from around her body, he studied her surreptitiously.

Too thin. Too pale. His eyes narrowed, and he looked away. One more night. He could put up with anything, knowing there was a time limit and he would have Delia back the way she'd been before.

The thin, high-strung woman dressing across the room from him had become a stranger.

He dressed quickly, wanting to get this final night over with. Slipping on his jeans, shirt and sweater, he smiled grimly at his reflection in the mirror. Industry people usually went to screenings right after work, so the dress code was casual. An actor—a "creative" person—could get away with anything. The more talented a person was, the more eccentricities were allowed. He and Delia could have probably come naked. All anyone cared about was whether the film worked.

Finished dressing, he took both their towels back to the steamy bathroom and hung them up. Walking quietly back into the room—he didn't want to say anything; both their tempers were on too short a fuse—he studied her quietly from his corner of the room.

She'd dressed in what he teasingly referred to as her Japanese coolie outfit. Full pants, cropped short. Soft cotton in a brilliant shade of royal blue, they had a matching tank top. But Delia was studying her reflection in the mirror, and he could tell she wasn't pleased.

Her arms are too thin. Gaunt.

She reached for the matching jacket and slipped it over her arms, effectively concealing them.

Her hair was drying naturally, wavy and full. She rushed through the minimum amount of makeup, then pushed herself back from the mirror and reached for her bag.

"Ready?" she asked.

He nodded. She walked toward him, her flat sandals noiseless against the deep carpeting. There was nothing in her way to trip her, but she stumbled against him, and he caught her, his fingers grasping her upper arms.

Even through the jacket he could feel her. Burning up.

Morgan could tell she sensed the change in him as soon as he touched her. She shrugged away and began to walk quickly toward the door.

"Let's go."

He grabbed the back of her jacket, and she stopped. Delia didn't resist as he pulled her slowly toward him, turning her so they were face-to-face. He slipped the jacket from her body slowly, his eyes never leaving hers. Her color was high, her eyes dilated. Why hadn't he seen it before? Because they hadn't been sleeping in the same bed.

"How long have you been sick?" he asked quietly.

She reached down quickly and grabbed her jacket, shrugging it on. "I can make it through—"

"How long!" He grabbed her upper arms and pulled her against him. A part of him hated what he was doing to her, but he wanted the truth. Morgan was tired of the lies between them.

She lowered her eyes, and he loosened his hold on her. "Just the last few days. But I slept in the car on the way home, and I feel better—"

He felt her forehead. Burning. He pushed her gently away from him so that she sat on the bed. "Like hell you do. I'm taking your temperature. Damn it, Delia, don't you care what you do to yourself?"

"We don't have time!" There was a tinge of panic to her voice as she struggled to sit up. "We have to be at the studio in—"

"No, we don't."

"Morgan!" Her eyes were wide, frightened. "I told Bob we'd—"

"I don't give a damn what you told Bob. We can spare a few minutes to take your temperature."

"*I have to be there!*" She shot up off the bed and crossed the room to the door.

He grabbed her, wrested her hand from the doorknob and half dragged, half carried, her to the bed. Setting her down, he kept his fingers entwined with hers as he forced her hands up over her head.

She began to cry. "Don't do this, Morgan."

He put his face against hers, his cheek against her hot skin. "I can't stand back and be a party to this. Delia, you're sick. You're in no condition to go tonight. Call it off."

Her body tensed. When she answered him, her voice was low and steady. "No. Get off me, Morgan."

"Call it off." He raised himself up so that he was looking down on her flushed face, but her hands were still captured by his.

"I can't." There was a note of desperation in her voice. "The vice-president of advertising is going to be there, all the publicity people— Morgan, I can't just cancel the screening! They need time to put the advertising campaign together. It has to be a Christmas release to qualify for—"

"I don't give a damn. They can all wait one week."

He could feel her temper starting to boil over, sensed it in the way her slight body began to shake. Her eyes were flashing angrily as she began to speak.

"Spoken like a spoiled, egotistical star! You're so used to getting everything your way you can't take anyone else into account. Damn you, Morgan, I'm going to this screening if I have to crawl there on my hands and knees."

"You're staying here." His tone was implacable.

"*No.*" She twisted her head and bit his hand. Hard.

He yelped in pain, and she used his moment of stunned surprise to vault off the bed and grab her bag. He was after her as she raced down the hall toward the front door. She almost opened it, but he came up behind her and pinned her to the door with his body.

"Don't do this, Delia." He was shocked to hear his voice tremble as all the emotion he'd been holding in for weeks and weeks threatened to break loose.

"Let me *go.*" She struggled against him, and he realized with blinding clarity it was useless to fight her. He believed her. Delia would crawl if that was what it took.

The film had become her life.

He decided to try one last time.

"Let him go, Delia," he said softly.

"Morgan, what are you—"

"Let James go. The film isn't going to bring him back." He hated saying the words, hated watching her face change as she stared up at him, stunned.

For a moment she almost crumpled. He watched the emotions play over her face, in her eyes. She closed them, as if unable to face the truth behind her actions. He felt her body relax, and he began to gather her into his arms. *Let him go.*

But she stiffened when she heard the knock on the door.

"Bob." She looked up at him, and he felt his insides twisting at the imploring expression on her face. "Please, Morgan. Just give me tonight. I won't ask for anything else. Ever."

He felt as if he were about to cry out, the emotions inside him were that strong. But he knew he couldn't stop her; she would hate him the rest of her life.

"Go on, then."

He let her go, and she reached for the doorknob. But as his words sunk in, she turned toward him slowly.

"Aren't you coming?"

The knock sounded again, more briskly this time. "Just a second, Bob!" Delia called out; then she turned toward him again. "We'll talk when we get back, Morgan."

He hated what he had to do. She was ill, in no condition to be going anywhere. His voice was soft when he answered her. "I won't be here when you get back, Delia."

Her eyes darkened as she looked at him, but he didn't look away from the pain in her expression. He tried one more time.

"Call it off." *Please*. He reached out and touched her face, his fingers cool against her fevered skin.

She looked away, and for a moment he sensed her wavering, torn between conflicting emotions. But he watched as the careful control settled over her features, and his heart felt as if it were splitting apart as he realized he'd lost.

She was going to go.

Delia stepped back, away from him, opened the door and walked out.

Chapter Twelve

Morgan slipped into the back row just as the lights went down in the small studio screening room. The only reason he'd let her go alone was because Bob was with her. She was in the third row, seated next to her godfather. He'd caught a glimpse of her blue jacket before the lights dimmed.

As the film began to roll and music filled the small theater, Morgan settled back in his seat and wondered what he would say to Delia when the film was over.

THE AIR CONDITIONING was too high. She was freezing. Her teeth had been chattering, and Bob had noticed, so he'd taken off his jacket and draped it around her shoulders.

But Delia still couldn't get warm.

She concentrated on the screen in front of her as her vision of the film began to unroll, frame by frame. The wild, untamed country was the perfect backdrop for the story, and Delia was suddenly fiercely glad she'd given James this last chance. The man and the land. His horses and his acting. Even if the film was flawed, this would be the performance James would be remembered for.

There was total silence when James first appeared on screen, and Delia studied him. *Perfect*. The first shot, his first words. She knew instinctively that the only way she'd ever be able to get through this evening was by looking at the film with totally dispassionate eyes. He wasn't James Wilde, her father, but a character in a film.

She shivered and pulled Bob's jacket closer around her. Though she was cold, she was sweating. The inside of her jacket felt wet. She sunk back into her seat, then started as she felt Bob put his arm around her and give her shoulders a gentle squeeze.

"James is wonderful. Delia, thank you for giving him this."

His words were her total undoing. She tried to study the screen again, but the images blurred.

The first sob tore out of her body, loud in the quiet theater. She covered her mouth with her hands as her shoulders began to shake. Bob tightened his hold on her, the gentle pressure a lifeline.

It was the hardest thing in the world, watching her father on the screen and knowing she'd never see him again. During the endless weeks of editing and dubbing, she'd pushed the knowledge of his death into the back of her mind, safely away from her deepest emotions. But seeing him on screen . . .

She bit down on her lip. *Stop*.

Delia made it through the first hour without breaking down. And she knew she'd been privileged to work on a masterpiece. Morgan and James set fire to each other, each actor making the other reach higher, dare more. And Delia watched both men she loved, her hand over her mouth, her eyes filled with tears.

By the time James's climactic scene was reached, she was a quaking bundle of nerves. It seemed like only a few days ago that she'd put her arm around her father's shoulder and helped him walk to his trailer. But even then she'd known. It was the scene of a lifetime. A scene most actors would kill for.

As James talked on about Mary Anne, his cinematic daughter, Delia felt her tenuous control snapping.

I can't take any more of this.

She put her hands over her face and began to sob.

WHEN MORGAN HEARD her first sob, he was halfway out of his chair before he remembered where he was. Slowly, every muscle in his body tensed, he lowered himself back into his seat.

His eyes had grown accustomed to the dark, and he found he was watching Delia far more than the film. Bob had his arm tightly around her thin shoulders, and Morgan relaxed slightly, satisfied she was safe.

He watched the film, uncomfortable with his performance on the screen. He hated watching himself. But he loved what was happening between James and every member of the cast.

You'll be remembered for this one, James. Delia had a right to be proud of what she'd pulled off. Against all odds.

Halfway through the film he heard her start to sob again. This time she didn't stop. The audience was perfectly quiet, utterly engrossed in the film but also respecting Delia's grief. Every single member of the audience knew what she'd gone through after her father's death to get this film ready in time for a Christmas release and Academy Award consideration.

No one was blaming her for breaking down now.

His chest hurt, and he realized he was taking each breath with her, feeling each catch in her throat. He wanted to jump out of his seat, run down the aisle and gather her up into his arms.

But he wanted her to have her moment of glory. She deserved it.

So he sat in the back of the darkened screening room, his eyes closed, hearing nothing but the sound of her crying.

THE LIGHTS CAME UP, and Delia wiped her hands over her wet face. The tears were streaming down her face; she couldn't make them stop.

People were coming by where she and Bob were seated.

"Beautiful film, Delia."

"Bob, it's going to be a hit. I can feel it."

"James was wonderful."

Voices swirled around her, but all she could think of was what an utter mess her life was.

Watching Morgan's last scene with Belinda, she'd remembered that day filming. He'd kissed her, given the scene to her, come back with her to Los Angeles and put up with eight weeks of insanity so that she could finish her dream.

What had she given him back? Half the time when she'd tumbled into bed, she hadn't even been aware of him. She'd snapped at him, stopped listening—she'd done everything wrong it was possible to do in a relationship.

So he was leaving her.

Her body felt unbearably tired, but she pushed herself out of her seat with an energy born out of desperation. *Call him. Maybe he hasn't left the house yet. Tell him how much you love him.*

Delia felt as if she were swimming through a sea of thick, humid air. She was no longer sweating; she felt as if she were being burned alive. There were too many bodies, too close. For an instant she wanted to claw her way through them and push to the door. There had to be a pay phone. If she could just hear Morgan's voice and tell him how very sorry she was—

She took one shaky step and immediately reached for the arm of the aisle seat in front of her. She wiped her hand across her forehead, and her fingers came away damp. Straightening, she took another step, then another.

Her legs weren't working. She looked out in front of her, into the sea of faces, and for an instant she thought she saw Morgan rushing down the aisle toward her, pushing people out of the way.

Then her legs gave way, and she staggered and fell.

SHE WOKE UP in an ambulance, Morgan's tense face close above hers. Delia tried to mouth a word, but she was so tired her eyes fluttered shut. It was enough to feel the warm pressure of his hand holding hers.

He didn't leave, she thought before she lapsed into unconsciousness.

When she opened her eyes again, she was in a hospital bed. The smell of antiseptic and alcohol was strong in her nostrils, and it made her want to gag.

"Morgan?" The word was barely a whisper.

She'd never seen such naked fear in anyone's eyes before. He was looking down at her face; then he lowered his head and kissed her forehead.

"You didn't go." Her speech was slurred from exhaustion.

"No. I couldn't— Delia, when I saw you fall—" He didn't continue, just kept looking at her face and holding her hand tightly.

She smiled, closing her eyes. "So silly."

"No, no it wasn't. I'm so sorry, Delia. I—I've never been good for you. I've always brought you pain, but I love you so much—"

"You're very good for me," she said quietly, remembering words said by a fire long ago.

She felt him move slightly away, and she

opened her eyes with the greatest amount of effort.

"Don't leave me. Please." The words were harsh and raw against her throat. Because no matter how well the film did, no matter how good she felt about giving it to her father, nothing mattered if Morgan didn't share it with her.

"I'm not going to leave," he said quickly.

There was someone else in the room. She could feel it. Turning her head, she saw a doctor standing on the other side of her bed.

She looked away from him, toward Morgan. She had to tell him now, all the reasons she loved him, before she fell asleep, before she lost her courage and was unable to apologize for the hell she'd put both of them through.

"I was wrong, Morgan. What I did." She tried to sit up but was astonished to find she had an IV running out of her arm. She searched for his face, caught his eyes and held them.

"I was wrong to go tonight—"

"Delia, stop—"

"It was stupid; you were right. I never meant to hurt you, but I've been awful—" She stopped talking as tears began to form in her eyes. She felt one slide down her cheek, and he wiped it away with a gentle finger. His hand trembled.

"Delia, the doctor's going to give you a shot to make you sleep. I don't want you to worry about anything."

"*Don't leave me.*" She clung to his hand, her eyes smarting. "Please, Morgan, stay with me."

"I'm not going anywhere." He leaned over

her bed and pressed his cheek gently against hers. "I'm going to stay here until you wake up. Then we'll talk about...everything. We have time now, darling. Everything's going to be fine. Perfect. This time we'll get it right." He managed a shaky smile. "Please don't worry."

She felt the cool alcohol on her inner elbow as the doctor prepared to give her the shot. And she gripped Morgan's hand as hard as she could.

Scared of needles, she looked at Morgan as she felt it prick her skin.

"I love you." It was the last thing she said before she fell asleep.

"HE'S HERE? Morgan Buckmaster! In this hospital?" The young blond nurse fairly quivered with excitement.

"In room 612. Delia Wilde. Remember, her father died just a few weeks ago? She collapsed at a screening, and he rushed her to the hospital. There's a rumor going around that they're engaged." The other nurse, a freckled redhead, was triumphant, having heard all the hospital gossip first.

"I'd *love* to see him! I wonder if he's as good-looking as he is in his films?"

"Better. A friend of mine saw him in Malibu." She lowered her voice. "Go on in there. Just pretend you're making rounds."

"Oh, I can't—"

"He's been there for almost six hours. I don't think he'll stay much longer."

Curiosity won out. "Okay. But I won't say a word. I just want to look at him."

She walked quickly down the hall. The hospital was quiet at this time of night. The door to 612 was slightly ajar, and she managed to squeeze inside without opening it any further.

Walking toward the bedside chart, the nurse looked up.

She shouldn't have worried. They were both asleep. Delia Wilde looked like a delicate princess, her dark hair fanned out over the hospital pillow. Her left arm had an IV in it, but her right hand was tightly clasped by Morgan.

Morgan Buckmaster. She studied his face quickly, not wanting to be caught in the room by the head nurse. He looked exhausted. Sitting in a chair by her side, he had her hand clasped in his, tightly, even though he slept.

But it was his face that captured her attention. More beautiful—in a masculine way—than she'd ever seen it on screen.

He looked utterly peaceful.

In so many of the pictures she'd seen, he'd seemed angry. Withdrawn. Or he'd smoldered quietly, promising a potent sexuality that made women go quietly crazy.

His features were illuminated by the nightlight next to Delia's bed. His head was tilted back against the white wall, his face relaxed. But it was his mouth that captured her attention.

He was smiling.

Epilogue

The surrounding peace and serenity couldn't have been more reflective of the way Delia felt inside.

Early-morning sunshine spilled over the red-wood deck of James's beach house. She gazed out over the ocean, totally content. Whatever had possessed her to think she and Morgan wouldn't make it?

Her picture had swept the Academy Awards. Best actor, Morgan Buckmaster. A special award for lifetime achievement given to James Wilde.

Best director, Delia Wilde.

It had been a night of wild celebrating, and she and Morgan had gone to every party in town. They'd danced the night away, driving home just before the sun rose.

But she couldn't sleep. She'd slipped out of her silk velvet backless cowl dress and put on her pink robe. Morgan had gone into the kitchen to make a pot of coffee.

So much had happened since the screening. She'd only been hospitalized for a week; then

Morgan had driven her back to his beach house.

They were married exactly one week later, at the ranch. It had been a quiet ceremony, with only Tom, Mary, Bob and a few other very close friends present.

He'd taken her away to Tahiti for a month. And it was while nestled in a private bungalow, alone that they really began to talk to each other.

In the beginning the only thing they'd been sure of was that they wanted to spend the rest of their lives together. There were still so many things she didn't know about Morgan, but he had laid out his soul to her while they walked some of the most beautiful beaches she'd ever seen. Away from the pressure, with time to be alone and themselves, the pieces had fallen into place.

He'd told her about his past, his upbringing, how he'd never felt he was worth anything, especially her love. She'd admitted how it had always felt to live a very public life as her father's daughter.

And in the end all of it faded away until it was just the two of them. There would be no more looking to the past—only to the future.

Her thoughts were interrupted as she heard the glass door behind her slide open.

"I thought I'd find you out here," he said, handing her a cup of coffee. He looked as wired as she felt and had changed out of his tuxedo into a pair of faded jeans. They stood by the redwood railing, gazing at the calm Pacific.

They drank their coffee in silence, grateful for

the respite from their partying. When Delia set her cup down, she leaned against the rail and looked up at him.

"So what do you want to do, Best Actor?" she teased. She'd been so proud of him when he'd bounded up on stage to accept his award. And she'd had tears in her eyes when he had thanked her father, the other members of the cast and at the very end, herself.

He took the last sip of his coffee before he answered her. "I just want to be with you."

She smiled, then linked her arms around his waist.

He traced her cheekbone with his finger. "So what do you want to do, Best Director?" he said softly.

"Funny. I just want to be with you, too."

His mouth quirked upward. "At last, we agree on something." He was silent for a minute, just holding her.

"Are you tired?" she asked.

"Not particularly."

She leaned back in the circle of his arms. "What do you want to do? I mean, right now. Make a decision, Morgan," she teased.

He kissed her cheek. "You're the director. Give me some directions."

She ran her hands up over his bare shoulders, up into the softness of his hair. "Give me a minute. I'm sure I'll think of something."

She teased him, touching him as long as possible, then finally exerted the gentlest of pressures and brought his lips close to hers.

"I think you should kiss me," she said softly.

It was a light, playful kiss, perfectly in tune to the moment.

When he lifted his head, she glanced up at him from underneath her lashes. "Do you make a habit of sleeping with all your directors?"

He swatted her bottom. "Just this one." He lowered his mouth and kissed her again.

She couldn't think when he broke the second kiss; could only rub her cheek against his chest.

Morgan's voice held a hint of laughter in it. "Where do you think this next scene should take place?"

"Oh, the bedroom. Unless you want to shock the neighbors."

"Not a very good policy, I think." He tilted her chin up with one of his fingers. "And what's my motivation?"

As he swept her up into his arms, she kissed the tip of his nose. "You have to answer that one." She looped her arms around his neck as he stepped inside the house and began to walk down the hall to their bedroom.

"My motivation? I love you, Delia Wilde. I love you very much."

She fought for a bold future
until she could no longer
ignore the...

ECHO OF THUNDER
MAURA SEGER

Author of **Eye of the Storm**

ECHO OF THUNDER is the love story of James
Callahan and Alexis Brockton, who forge a union that
must withstand the pressures of their own desires and the
challenge of building a new television empire.

Author Maura Seger's writing has been described by
Romantic Times as having a "superb blend of historical
perspective, exciting romance and a deep and abiding
passion for the human soul."

You're invited to accept 4 books and a surprise gift Free!

Acceptance Card

Mail to: **Harlequin Reader Service®**

In the U.S.
2504 West Southern Ave.
Tempe, AZ 85282

In Canada
P.O. Box 2800, Postal Station A
5170 Yonge Street
Willowdale, Ontario M2N 6J3

YES! Please send me 4 free Harlequin American Romance® novels and my free surprise gift. Then send me 4 brand new novels as they come off the presses. Bill me at the low price of $2.25 each —an 11% saving off the retail price. There are no shipping, handling or other hidden costs. There is no minimum number of books I must purchase. I can always return a shipment and cancel at any time. Even if I never buy another book from Harlequin, the 4 free novels and the surprise gift are mine to keep forever.

154 BPA-BPGE

Name _____ (PLEASE PRINT)

Address _____ Apt. No. _____

City _____ State/Prov. _____ Zip/Postal Code _____

This offer is limited to one order per household and not valid to present subscribers. Price is subject to change.   ACAR-SUB-1

Readers rave about
Harlequin American Romance!

"The stories are great from beginning to end."
—*M.W., Tampa, Florida*

"...excellent new series...I am greatly impressed."
—*M.B., El Dorado, Arkansas*

"I am delighted with them...can't put them down."
—*P.D.V., Mattituck, New York*

"Thank you for the excitement, love and adventure your books add to my life. They are definitely the best on the market."
—*J.W., Campbellsville, Kentucky*

Names available on request.

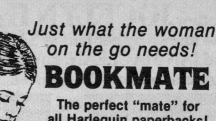
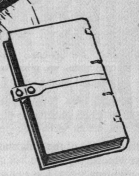

Author JOCELYN HALEY,
also known by her fans as SANDRA FIELD and JAN MACLEAN, now presents her eighteenth compelling novel.

DREAM of DARKNESS

With the help of the enigmatic Bryce Sanderson, Kate MacIntyre begins her search for the meaning behind the nightmare that has haunted her since childhood.

Together they will unlock the past and forge a future.